Nicholas – The Legend Begins

a coming-of-age novel based on the real Saint Nicholas

Joe Dodridge
© 2020

joedodridge.com

Nicholas – The Legend Begins

a coming-of-age novel based on the real Saint Nicholas

Joe Dodridge
joedodridge.com

Copyright © 2020
ISBN: 9798677369421

All rights reserved. Don't copy it! You might have a cool haircut and I don't copy it. So, don't copy my book.

Cover image: used with permission

Nicholas – The Legend Begins

Table of Contents

1 – Escape -- 7
2 – Shock --- 19
3 – Alexander --- 31
4 – The Barn -- 39
5 – Jailed -- 53
6 – Deceived -- 63
7 – The Spiral -- 77
8 – Redeemed -- 90
9 – The Return --- 107
10 – Trouble --- 117
11 – Monday -- 130
12 – Tuesday Morning, Payment 1 ------------------------ 140
13 – Tuesday Night -- 150
14 – Wednesday Morning, Payment 2 ---------------------- 158
15 – The Plan -- 169
16 – Wednesday Night --------------------------------------- 177
17 – Thursday Morning, Payment 3 ----------------------- 189
18 – The Legend Begins ------------------------------------ 197

About the Author --- 200

Nicholas – The Legend Begins

1 – Escape

 The sun was just about to rise when Nicholas first realized he might be getting tired. The moment immediately before sunrise is a peaceful, yet lonely and chilly time - even in late September. The easterly sky slowly lit with its faint morning glow, and the hazy place where the earth meets that sky began to dance with subtle hues of purple and orange. Birds weren't yet chirping and the calm weather of the night made the sea seem as smooth as a solid piece of ancient Parthian glass. It was as if every person in the world had disappeared and Nicholas was the only one left.
 He could hardly believe he spent the entire night alone on his boat. He had made it through the night only one other time all by himself. Nicholas's boat was a simple sailboat. Of course he knew how to sail, practically everyone in Myra knew how to sail. Now, it wouldn't be wise to sail too far out into the Mediterranean Sea, and it certainly wouldn't be wise to sail by yourself in any kind of weather except clear, calm weather. People sailed by themselves often – especially if they were fishing or traveling. Nicholas wasn't fishing and he wasn't traveling. He was escaping.

Mind you, Nicholas wasn't escaping from anything or anyone. He wasn't trying to go anywhere. He was just escaping in his own mind – the way one might escape in a good book or a bath or a favorite drink. The sea was Nicholas's book – his way to think, be still, and drown out the worries of life.

You might think that Nicholas had a tough life, with the need to escape and all. On the contrary, he was given more in life than you or I dream of.

Most people would agree that Nicholas was a handsome, 19-year-old man. He was slightly tall, had blond hair and deep blue eyes. He was not only well educated, but also naturally smart. He knew how to carry himself in a group of adults and had all of the physical and personal traits that made other people want to be around him.

Nicholas was the only child of Epiphanius and Johanna, wealthy sellers of fine textiles. Nicholas's parents had a very nice house with a courtyard (fairly unusual for where they lived). Epiphanius employed a handful of men in his business and Johanna worked hard at home, even though they could certainly afford to pay people to do the work for her. In fact, most people of their status had slaves, but Nicholas's parents did not agree with the idea, so they did not have them.

Originally from the town of Patara, Epiphanius and Johanna wed when they were just late teenagers. They were neighbors growing up – Epiphanius had a strong work ethic, even as a boy, coupled with an overwhelming desire to be fair and just. As a girl, Johanna was very compassionate. Her heart broke when other people's hearts broke and she was always so willing to give what she had to help someone else.

The story of his parents' engagement is one that Nicholas had heard told so many times, sometimes he wondered if perhaps he was even there.

"Johanna, I have something I would like you to hear – and it comes with a question," Epiphanius said nervously, just barely 18 years old.

"Epiphanius, I always want to hear what you have to say. Unless, of course, you are going to remind me about the time I baked you bread and burned it, or if you are going to try and sing. I absolutely don't want to hear that!" Johanna replied, always having a way of lightening a moment.

Hardly hearing what she said and clearing his throat, Epiphanius proceeded with his rehearsed speech, "I may not be old and wise, and I may not be rich and strong. But, I want to grow old with you, learn the wisdom that comes with being loved by you, gain riches in your beauty, and build strength in your devotion and compassion. Johanna, will you marry me?"

Usually one for a quick-witted reply, Johanna could only whisper a barely audible, "Yes," and that cemented their love and devotion to each other for the rest of their lives.

Theirs was a love that was strong and unbreakable. Despite marrying young, they did not have Nicholas until a dozen years after marrying. Johanna was afraid that she would never have a child. Despite Epiphanius's love and constant reassurance, her barrenness caused her much grief in the first years of their marriage.

All of Johanna's brothers and sisters had children. Even Epiphanius's only sister, who no one thought would ever marry, found some type of love and gave birth to twins. Barrenness was difficult on Johanna's faith, as it has been for generations of barren women before and after her. It was only after about seven or eight years into this trial that she began to find peace in her barrenness. She often reassured herself by thinking, "If this is the lot that God has given me, then this is the lot that I accept."

Then, in what Johanna describes as a miracle, she conceived and gave birth to Nicholas. By this point in their life, they were not yet rich, and his birth and the barrenness that led up to it grounded Johanna in her faith and in her life. She didn't take anything for granted and counted even the smallest things in life as blessings. She tried so hard not to spoil Nicholas as a child, but when a mother goes through so much grief and trouble to have one child, it is difficult not to spoil him.

Nevertheless, she tried her best. She was blessed by God with a loving husband and what would be their only child.

Epiphanius loved his wife and his son. If there existed such an award given to the father who best balanced a successful business with time and devotion to his family, then Epiphanius would win that award.

He often liked to take Nicholas, just the two of them, to his cabin in the mountains. It was on these getaways that Epiphanius and Nicholas had long talks – talks about life and faith and love. Epiphanius was proud of his son, Nicholas, even if he sometimes thought his mother made him a little soft. Marrying young, Epiphanius felt like he had missed out on the last few years of his childhood. So, he allowed Nicholas to be a boy probably a little longer than he should have. Now that Nicholas was 19 years old, Epiphanius had only just started to train Nicholas in the textile business.

Epiphanius was proud of his business and worked hard to develop relationships throughout their province, Lycia. He started trading in textiles when he moved his wife and son to Myra fifteen years ago and quickly began partnering with a local businessman, Alexander. Myra was a perfect location – a favorite stopping point of ships heading into the eastern reaches of the Roman Empire – especially ships from Macedonia, Asia, and even Rome itself.

The distribution of textiles might not sound like much today, but it was a big business in the late third century. The main fabrics of the day were wool and linen. Sheep and goats for wool were primarily grown west of Myra – in Greece and Rome. Flax plants for linen were primarily grown east and south of Myra – in Syria and Egypt. So, with its centralized location and port on the Mediterranean Sea, all it took was a hard-working, honest businessman like Epiphanius to capitalize on the textile trade. His work ethic, along with his partner Alexander's contacts throughout the entire Roman Empire, made the business quite successful.

Just beginning to learn about the business, Nicholas had never realized all of the relationships that it took to make money. Now, as a new adult, Nicholas was beginning to appreciate the hard work that his dad had put into the business and also to appreciate the advantage that a well-connected partner like Alexander could offer.

Nicholas had nearly everything he could ask for and everything money could buy. His life was easy – money and food and education and friends. His parents were well-known and respected, so Nicholas was also well-known and respected. He even liked a girl – a young woman named Aemilia. Aemilia's father, Stephen, was also a wealthy merchant, trading in pottery – particularly Corinthian pottery which was highly sought after throughout the eastern Roman Empire. Well, actually, he used to be wealthy. His business was going through a bit of a hard time. He had some debts and was barely making his debt payments while still trying to maintain his business. Their debt and struggling business worried Stephen and his wife, Faustina, causing a strain on their marriage and stress in their lives.

A life of plenty, a life of respect, and a girl. Nicholas didn't seem to need to escape, yet here he was. Nicholas watched the sun peak up over the eastern edge of the sea. Yawning, he reached down to find that his water flask was empty. He would have to fill that craving later – a silly example of how something so basic as thirst gets the best of both the wealthy and the poor. For now, it didn't matter. Nicholas was alone in the world, alone in his thoughts, and soon drifting asleep. He thought he heard the morning's first bird's cry, and then his eyes wandered shut and he slept.

It's obvious that Nicholas forgot today was Sunday. His parents would be in church and they would expect him there too. To say they expected him there makes it sound like he didn't want to go. On the contrary, Nicholas believed the faith of his parents, just perhaps had not completely made it his own faith. He certainly wasn't a bad person and his wealth had only just barely spoiled him. He enjoyed learning about God and Jesus, and he thought there must be something to it – he just wasn't sure. Some people in Nicholas's church thought that he might make a good priest someday. Nicholas didn't think, however, that one should become a priest just because other people thought you'd be good at it.

It wasn't the best time, however, to be a Christian – that wouldn't come until Emperor Constantine converted to Christianity in about 20 years. More accepted than perhaps 200 years before, the late third century was still a trying time. Emperor Diocletian, while not yet persecuting Christians to the extent that he soon would, decreed edicts requiring Christians to "be more Roman." They could still worship in church, but some people stopped attending church out of fear for their safety. Nicholas didn't worry, though. In his mind, his family was safe – money has a way of providing a false sense of security. And, after all, Diocletian seemed worlds away from Myra, off on one of his conquests in some distant land.

For now, Nicholas slept the morning away. Sleep has its own way of providing escape. The moments of sleep provide us escape from the conscious stresses of our day. For Nicholas, his escape was less about running from something and more about running to something. Escape allowed his mind to put together life's puzzle pieces and to plan for the future. He had so much to process about his role in the business. Would his father send him on one of Alexander's buying journeys to Alexandria or Thessalonica? Maybe his father would train him in the art of dyeing materials or the skills needed to negotiate deals.

A few hours into the new morning, Nicholas awoke to the sharp realization that today was Sunday and he was supposed to be in church. As if God was punishing him for his sin, there was no wind to carry his little boat back to shore, so Nicholas began feverishly rowing.

The closer he got to shore, the nearby rocks and trees swallowed up the not-to-distant mountains. Summer was just turning into Autumn, so there was no snow yet on the mountains. The weather in Myra was quite pleasant year-round, but those mountains climb in elevation quickly enough that they support snow throughout the winter. Nicholas's family cabin was fairly high in the mountains, allowing it to get that snow – something Nicholas's dad especially liked when he needed his own escape.

Myra was located along the northeastern Mediterranean Sea. Blessed with a moderate seaside climate, Myra never got too hot or too cold. Myra was situated on a strip of land squeezed between the sea and the mountains. Truly beautiful and scenic, a person could be boating in the sun's warmth one day and then trekking through a half-foot of snow several thousand feet up the mountain the very next day. The town itself was quite large for the area – later in Nicholas's life it would become the capital of Lycia. Most of Myra's people were of Greek descent, though its shipping business gave it somewhat of a cosmopolitan population. With a strong tradition of Greek culture, Myra contained a mix of Greek temples, Roman temples, and Christian churches.

As Nicholas's arms grew more and more tired, his thoughts turned to Aemilia. He met Aemilia several years ago, probably when he was ten and she was only eight. Their families ran in the same social circles and would often attend the same parties and festivals. Aemilia was the youngest of three daughters – all close in age, separated by only two-and-a-half years. Nicholas found no interest in her when he was a boy, but things sure seemed to be changing as he got older.

His earliest memory of Aemilia was when Nicholas was ten years old, during a party his parents hosted to get to know the community better. Alexander always encouraged Epiphanius to host these parties. On the one hand, they were a great tool to expand business. On the other hand, Alexander talked Epiphanius into being the host so that Epiphanius and Johanna had to do all of the work and pay for the party!

"Be careful, you don't quite have that knot tied right." Aemilia, whom Nicholas had never met, was honestly trying to warn Nicholas that his dog was about to escape. Nicholas only had his dog, Neptune, for two weeks. It was one of Alexander's ideas for Nicholas's family to show the town that they were well-off by owning a dog, and Nicholas had really taken a liking to Neptune. While his parents didn't worship Roman gods, Alexander convinced them that their dog needed a good Roman name (after all, Neptune was the god of the seas and the merchants they traded with would appreciate a dog named Neptune).

"I know what I'm doing," ten-year-old Nicholas replied, not really knowing anything, but not wanting to appear dumb before a girl.

"Well, I'm not trying to tell you what to do or how to do it, I just figured that you wouldn't like your dog running away."

"He's not going to get a-," which is all Nicholas could reply as his parent's new sign of prosperity ran through the party in the courtyard and out the gate.

With that, Nicholas immediately ran after Neptune, while Aemilia turned and ran in the opposite direction. "A lot of help she is," Nicholas thought. "She can offer advice but she can't pitch in and help when I really need it."

Nicholas ran out the gate and caught a glimpse of Neptune cutting left down the street. He ran as fast as his young legs could carry him, but Neptune had more energy and even more motivation. "We should have named him Aergia and maybe I could catch him," Nicholas thought, because Aergia was the Greek god of laziness.

It wasn't long before Nicholas couldn't keep up with the dog and it turned one too many corners for him to know which way to continue running. Dejected because he lost the new brother he never had, he started walking back home, trying to think up the right thing to tell his parents.

With his story rehearsed and his tears real, Nicholas entered through the courtyard gate and slowly walked to his parents. "Mom, Dad, I have some terrible news." And, just before he could get the next words out through his sobbing, he looked past his parents and saw Aemilia holding Neptune.

Forgetting that he was tearfully about to deliver news to his parents, he ran over to Aemilia, who had just more securely tied Neptune's knot. Nicholas barely heard her talk about dogs and their attraction to butcher markets. Instead, he was just happy to have back his new furry friend.

"Thank you," Nicholas said, hoping she couldn't tell his face was tear-stained.

"You're welcome. My name is Aemilia. What's yours?"

"My parents call me Nicholas, but you can call me Nick."

Now they were older and Aemilia was 17 and much more interesting than when she was eight. Aemilia had an unassuming beauty that was both inward and outward. All it took was one meaningful conversation with her to realize that she loved leading a compassionate life and had a maturity about her that was uncommon for her age. Outwardly, she was beautiful. Not in the way that Roman temple workers tried to display beauty, but rather a modest beauty – keeping her long, blond hair neat, her modest dresses crisp (modest in discretion, not necessarily in price), and wearing a smile that directed all eyes to her room-brightening face.

Nicholas would regularly take walks past Aemilia's house just to hope to see her and stop and talk. Of course, Aemilia had the same sort of feelings toward Nicholas, though neither one of them was clever enough to figure out how to express it. She was a strong and wise young woman. Though she had opinions (even about dog knots), she wasn't one to make sure everyone else knew about them. While she was the youngest of three girls, she wasn't the traditional baby of her family. Perhaps that had something to do with all three sisters being so close in age.

Nicholas had never really given any thought as to why he was attracted to Aemilia instead of her older sisters, Diantha and Iris. Diantha was a typical oldest child, generally responsible and concerned about learning her family's pottery business from a young age. She didn't have much interest in boys and that suited Nicholas just fine. She and Nicholas were the closest in age, but she always acted like she was much older than Nicholas.

Nicholas didn't usually act spoiled by his parents' riches, but Diantha liked to cast him in that role when she had the chance.

If anyone was outwardly pursuing Nicholas, it was the second sister, Iris. Iris took interest in Nicholas every time they were together, but then Iris also took interest in just about every other boy she was in a room with. Iris didn't have much use for learning the family's business. Her world was carefree and playful, certainly not serious like her older sister Diantha's world.

Over the years at family and community events, Nicholas found himself playing with Aemilia, and then as the years went by, having deep, meaningful conversations with Aemilia. Her family was also Christian, so she and Nicholas would talk about faith and Emperor Diocletian and life and business. Nicholas understood Amelia and provided an unrestricted outlet for her opinions and ideas. Aemilia understood Nicholas and loved to sit beside him when his head and mouth escaped from reality while he talked about the future and about what it might be.

Trying to get to church, Nicholas rowed so hard that he crashed onto the shore and nearly tumbled into the shallow water. His goal was to get the boat up on the shore as far as possible so that he would be as dry as possible whenever he got to church. Nicholas was not the kind of rich kid who threw around money or didn't value money, but he was in a hurry and he did not even take the time to tie up his boat or to put it in a place where people wouldn't bother it. "On this one occasion," he thought, "If someone takes my boat, then I have the means to buy a new one. I have to get to church before my dad lectures me about responsibility and reputation."

Nicholas ran across the beach, over the rocks, and up the small hill to the road. From there Nicholas had about a half-mile run to church. He tried to get there as quickly as he could, all while feeling the morning's sun beating down on him. Despite the fact that the temperature was not too warm, he was sweating and thought what a sight he would be and what a smell he would smell when he finally got to church. As he ran down the road toward the church, he hardly even noticed the beggar he passed on the side of the road or the smoke in the opposite side of town.

If running to church as fast as possible was one end of the spectrum, the opposite end was walking into the church as quietly and slowly as he could – all while out of breath. Nicholas wanted to make as little of a scene as possible. He was often late to church, and his parents were never too happy about it. Didn't they realize that he was 19 years old and that he could make his own decisions? Nevertheless, he wanted to please his parents and do what was right.

As he slowly opened the door to the church, he tried to sneak into the back row. He hoped that people wouldn't notice him – he had done it before and usually only one or two people saw.

This time was different. It seemed as if every eye was on him as he tried to slide into the back of the church. Even Papa Antony, the priest, was looking at him as Nicholas quietly sat in the back, fixing his hair and acting like he wasn't out of breath. (At this time priests were called "Papa" and didn't yet have the title of "Father.")

Papa Antony is best described as a jolly man. Jolly can mean lots of things, and if you're picturing someone slightly short and a little overweight, then you've nailed a mental picture of Papa Antony. He had an infectious laugh, a laugh that generated from deep within his gut – actually from deep within his soul.

Much to Nicholas's horror, Papa Antony started walking toward him. He thought, "What is he doing? This is the middle of a church service! I certainly hope that he is not going to lecture me on getting to church on time. I certainly don't need to come to church every Sunday if I'm just going to be embarrassed."

But, as Papa Antony approached, Nicholas noticed an unexpected look on his face. It wasn't quite disapproval and it wasn't quite disappointment. His face had a look of sadness and sorrow.

Papa Antony neared Nicholas, and Nicholas braced for what he figured was going to be his own personal sermon. His eyes quickly scanned the room, and he didn't see his parents. He decided that they must be out looking for him. He had been late before, so why should they bother with looking for him this time?

Papa Antony bent down toward Nicholas's ear. The entire congregation watched (while also trying to look like they were not watching). And with four simple words, Nicholas's life changed forever. Papa Antony whispered to him, "Your parents are dead."

2 – Shock

"Nicholas, I'm so sorry to tell you, son, but your parents have died," Papa Antony spoke softly. He was accustomed to comforting the afflicted, but this seemed even a little too much for him.

"There was a fire in the linen barn last night – your father went to put it out – your mother went with him." Papa Antony paused between sentences, allowing the weight of his words to sink into Nicholas. "They probably shouldn't have gone in. Others were there to help, but it was too late. I'm so sorry."

Nicholas could only manage to hear key words – died, fire, parents. Could he have helped? What if he never would have gone out on that stupid boat? Why would his parents rush in? How could this happen? How could God let this happen?

With the idea of having a church service lost in the weight of the moment, one by one members of the congregation filed by Nicholas. Most offered their sorrow and some offered to help however they could. Nicholas couldn't even remember who was there or what they said. The priest said something about his parents being in heaven, but heaven seemed too far away from Nicholas to matter. A nice older couple in the church offered to walk Nicholas home. He doesn't remember saying yes or no, but the next thing he realized was that he was walking home with them by his side.

Approaching the house, Neptune greeted Nicholas at the courtyard gate. Much slower than he was as a puppy and oblivious to the day's events, Neptune leaped up onto Nicholas, licking his face. Nicholas welcomed the attention and rejected it at the same time. He was numb and didn't know how to think or how to react.

Nicholas walked toward the front door. A small number of people were waiting inside his house. Aemilia was there with her mother, Faustina. Alexander was there (he was alone because he wasn't married – he was married to his work). There was also a handful of neighbors.

"Oh Nick, I'm so sorry!" Aemilia sobbed as she burst out the front door. Aemilia had been waiting at his house ever since news first broke of the fire. At first, she feared that Nicholas was in the linen barn too, but was reassured when she found out that he wasn't there.

"Nicholas, words can't even begin to explain…" Alexander, his dad's business partner, muttered as he couldn't even finish his own sentence.

"Thanks," was all Nicholas could respond to Alexander. It didn't even make sense as a response, but he didn't know what to say.

He turned toward Aemilia. In an instant it felt like she was all he had in this world. She instinctively put her hands out toward him and he fell into her arms sobbing. He sobbed and he sobbed as they sat down together. He muttered incomprehensible things about death and numbness and fright and love and confusion. Aemilia ran her hands through his thick, blond hair and Nicholas cried. After a few minutes and half-hearted condolences, Nicholas's neighbors left, followed by Alexander. With Aemilia's mother staying busy in Nicholas's kitchen, he cried and lightly slept in Aemilia's arms for the next couple of hours.

Aemilia's head raced as Nicholas leaned against her. He was sleeping and sobbing. She sobbed too. "Imagine losing my parents!" she thought. Aemilia's heart was so big and her empathy was so great that she could hardly bear the weight of the moment.

Aemilia was in love with Nicholas. She knew it without being previously conscious of it. Her sisters weren't yet married, so she hadn't really given much thought of marriage herself. She and Nicholas had never shared their true feelings with each other, but in this moment, she had absolute clarity about how she felt toward him.

Among her thoughts, Amelia remembered the day that she first realized there was something different about her feelings toward Nicholas. She was 15 – it was just about two years ago. Nicholas, Aemilia, and her two sisters were sent to the market by their parents to purchase fruit for that evening's party. Naturally, Diantha took the lead and had to carry the money and Iris wouldn't stop flirting with Nicholas as they walked to the market.

"12 libras of apples, please," Diantha exclaimed, being sure to place the order before anyone else could beat her to it.

"One dupondius," exclaimed the merchant as he weighed out twelve libras of apples. (A dupondius was worth about one-eighth of a denarius.)

"Here you go," said Diantha, handing over the coin. Her father had given her three just in case. The merchant took the coin and began to place the apples in Diantha's basket – she had to carry that too.

"Just a minute!" exclaimed Nicholas. "What are you trying to do here? Dishonesty in scales is against the law!"

"What are you accusing me of, boy?" the merchant replied. "Do you think that 12 libras weighs differently for your rich blood than it does for mine? Take your apples and go!"

Not to be intimidated, Nicholas exclaimed, "There's no way that's 12 libras of apples. Not unless you grow apples filled with rocks!"

By this time a small number of people gathered around the merchant's table. Trying to keep from making a scene and knowing that he was about to be caught in a lie, the merchant said, "Here, take some extra apples. There's nothing wrong with my scale, but take the apples and get out of here!"

Nicholas wouldn't let it go, though. He spoke loudly, for all to hear, "This man is trying to cheat us. He is cheating everyone. His scale must be wrong!"

With those words, a nearby merchant brought his scale and weighed out the apples. Then another merchant found a piece of metal attached to the bottom of the fruit merchant's scale, allowing him to overcharge his customers. In no time at all, a local soldier came and arrested the man. For their help, the soldier gave the teens their apples for free.

From that moment, Aemilia knew there was something different about Nicholas. She was attracted to his honesty and his stand for justice. He wasn't the spoiled brat that Diantha painted him to be and he wasn't the flirt that Iris wished he would be. He was Nicholas, a boy unlike any other she knew, and she was attracted to that.

Nicholas woke up in the early afternoon. He was a little confused and his consciousness hadn't quite caught up to the pain that his subconsciousness felt. In the matter of a moment, however, he remembered that his parents were gone and that he was with Aemilia who was comforting him.

"Aemilia, what am I going to do?" Nicholas asked, not really expecting an answer.

"You'll get through this, Nick. And I'll be here to help you." Aemilia was blessed with abundant servings of both wisdom and faith, especially rare for a 17-year-old girl.

"My parents are gone. I'm only 19. How will I live without them? I don't know my father's business. How can I run it?"

"Nick, you have many people who love you and support you. You don't need to have all of the answers. Alexander will help with the business. You have questions that can't be answered yet and that don't need to be answered yet."

Nicholas looked at her, hearing her response but continuing in his own thoughts.

"They are too young to be gone. My parents are good people – they help a lot of people. Why would God do this? Why would he take them from me? Why would he take away the life that they had? Why?"

Before Aemilia could think of the best response, Nicholas was sobbing. All she could do was whisper that everything was going to be alright.

As they sat there in silence, interrupted by an occasional sob, people started to gather once again at Nicholas's house. First, Papa Antony and his wife, Caecilia showed up (during the late third century, it was still common for priests to be married). He wanted to minister to Nicholas and to plan for the memorial service tomorrow, on Monday afternoon.

Papa Antony walked over to where Nicholas and Aemilia were sitting.

"God has a plan, even when we don't know it or understand it," Papa Antony said, trying to console Nicholas but more or less reciting the same phrases he told everyone else in times like this.

"I don't understand how God could do this," Nicholas numbly replied, wondering if Papa Antony ever really had to believe the seemingly empty words he was offering.

"Life is temporary." Papa Antony began speaking with a little more compassion. "Suffering and pain happen to us all – that is why we have a God and a Savior. It is less about God allowing the pain and more about God providing the comfort. We live in a fallen world with sinful people. That is why our hope is an eternal hope – a hope that has promises beyond this temporary life that we are given.

"Your parents' faith was strong – and I believe they are in heaven. You can trust that. You can place your hope in that."

"My parents being in heaven gives me nothing but pain here on earth," Nicholas said. He actually couldn't quite believe the words that were coming out of his mouth – exposing his lack of faith and his hurt. Papa Antony was wise enough to recognize it as pain, so he chose not to engage Nicholas further today in a discussion of faith and suffering. Instead, they began talking about the memorial service.

Soon after Papa Antony arrived, Nicholas's friend, Rufus, stopped by. Rufus and Nicholas had been friends since practically the first day Nicholas moved to Myra. Rufus was a loyal friend to Nicholas, although not always the most levelheaded and mature. Nicholas was definitely the leader of the two, often talking Rufus out of some dumb idea and balancing a logical consistency with Rufus's often irrational impulsiveness.

Rufus was appropriately named for his bright red hair. He also had a pretty fair complexion. He was not so pale that he looked sick, but paler than most people. Rufus was also a touch on the short side.

Rufus wasn't from the same side of town where Nicholas and Aemilia lived. Rufus's family worked hard for the little bit that they had. As a result, Rufus wasn't as educated as Nicholas and for the last few years he had to work to help out his parents. That wasn't all bad, however, because even at his relatively young age Rufus was very adept at building things. He figured that one day he might use those skills to build a house, but for now he was training to work with his rough and crass father in loading and unloading ships.

All those years ago Nicholas met Rufus when Nicholas's father was scouting out a place near the bay to store his new linen supply. Nicholas would accompany his father around town, on the one hand trying to stay out of trouble and on the other hand looking for adventure. When his father was scouting out one particular barn that didn't work out, Nicholas was outside, exploring the windows and doors. That's where he met a young Rufus, holding a stick, pretending to fish. Nicholas was just five years old and Rufus was four. Nicholas wasn't sure if there were any fish in that mud puddle and he didn't see any string on Rufus's stick, but it looked like fun to him anyway. As it turned out, they saw each other frequently after that, as

Nicholas's dad often employed Rufus's dad to handle linen. Their friendship grew over the years.

Rufus was pretty dumbstruck about Nicholas's parents' death. They had always been so kind to him. "Nick, I'm so sorry about your parents. I couldn't believe it when I heard. I thought there must be some mistake."

"Thanks, Rufus. I'm not quite sure I believe it either. I feel like I'm going to wake up and all of this will have just been a dream – a nightmare."

"I had to stop by the barn on my way here – just to see it with my own eyes. Some people I talked to there said the fire was just so intense."

"I should have been there, Rufus. Maybe I could have helped them put it out. I was on the boat last night – how dumb!"

"There's nothing you could have done, Nick. Don't beat yourself up."

"I want to go see the barn. Will you go with me to see it?" Nicholas paused. "I know you already went. You don't have to go if you don't want to."

"Sure, I'll go, though there's not much to see. When do you want to go?"

"I suppose we should go the day after the funeral. Papa Antony and I are working on a memorial service for tomorrow and it is going to be dark soon today."

"I want to go too," chimed in Aemilia.

"OK, thanks Aemilia," Nick replied. He was appreciative to have both her and Rufus with him. Papa Antony meant well, but he didn't know Nicholas like his friends did.

Papa Antony and Nicholas continued preparing for the memorial service. They decided that it would be easiest on Nicholas to have it in the church. Aemilia's mother, Faustina, offered to organize a meal at her home. Epiphanius and Johanna were well-respected in the community and wealthy – there would certainly be a lot of people at the service and the meal. Aemilia's parents' house was a very nice house, especially for Myran standards. But, while Nicholas's house stood alone, Aemilia's house was located in a string of homes, more like row homes. They were next to each other, lined up one by one, mostly sharing common walls. Aemilia's house was built in more of a Roman style, while Nicholas's house was built in more of a Greek style. Though Aemilia's family had a very nice house, they didn't have the luxury of a courtyard like Nicholas's house had.

Aemilia's parents, Stephen and Faustina, didn't exactly have very much money at the time to provide the meal. Always optimistic like her daughter, Faustina was pretty confident that she could find a way to make it work. As already mentioned, Stephen and Faustina were having a tough time financially. The pottery business wasn't going so well and Aemilia's dad couldn't figure out why. People were still buying pottery, even fine Corinthian pottery. They just weren't buying it from him. In fact, several of his key associates in other Roman cities stopped trading with him. It was quite an odd and stressful situation; it was like someone was working against him. Though he was a Christian, Stephen's darkest doubts made him even consider paying an offering at a local Roman temple to see if it helped.

They hadn't shared it with their daughters, but they were really concerned about possibly losing their home. Faustina had recently been turning her thoughts toward her daughters getting married, as that would provide the best security for each of them. Diantha wasn't exactly on her way to marriage, though Faustina was encouraging her to begin to think along those lines. Iris was certainly interested in boys, and Faustina figured she might have the best chance of getting married first, though she was worried about the type of husband Iris might attract. As for Aemilia, Faustina really hoped that Nicholas might become her husband. But since Aemilia was the youngest daughter and Nicholas was among the wealthiest possible suitors, she was afraid to press too hard and possibly mess up the young love that they might be developing.

While Papa Antony, Nicholas, Aemilia, and Faustina were talking, Alexander came again to Nicholas's house. Nicholas remembered him being there that morning.

"Thank you for being here, Alexander. You have been a good friend to my father."

"I have known your father for many years, Nicholas. He was a good man and will be greatly missed throughout the entire province of Lycia."

"What about the business, Alexander? I have only begun to learn about it. I don't know if I can step into my father's shoes."

"All in due time, Nicholas. You can trust me; I will keep things going for now. I had a trip scheduled to Thessalonica next month, but I will cancel it and focus on getting everything figured out."

"What about the fire? Did we lose much of the supply?"

"I'm afraid we lost quite a bit, Nicholas. I still have to determine exactly how much, but it was quite a blow. However, don't worry about it. Let me figure it out. You mourn your parents and I'll take care of the business."

"Thank you, Alexander. I owe you so much."

This is where our story starts to take a twist. You've probably guessed by now that Nicholas's story deals with overcoming his parents' death. While that was a major life-shaping event in Nicholas's life, it is only a small piece of the overall picture.

Perhaps you've guessed that this will be a story about Nicholas's faith – how he grew from the faith of his parents into his own faith. Just like his parents' death is an important part of the picture, his faith is also an important part of the picture, but not the main narrative that drives who Nicholas becomes.

It was Alexander who would be the catalyst in transforming Nicholas into the legend that he is today. Alexander, the business partner. Alexander, the father's friend. Alexander, the comforter. Alexander, the one who promised Nicholas that he would take care of the business.

However, lest you think that this is a story about the surrogate-father Alexander taking the orphaned, man-child Nicholas under his wing, let me set that straight right now.

You see, Alexander hadn't been quite forthright with Epiphanius over the years. While Epiphanius was a good, honest businessman, he trusted his partner Alexander a little too blindly. Soon into their partnership, Alexander figured a way that he could take a little more than half of the profits without Epiphanius knowing. It started small, just a few dozen denarii here or there. But, as their business grew and Alexander's business relationships grew with it, Alexander was able to make deals in far-off places like Thessalonica and Alexandria and Nicomedia – deals that filled his pockets with money that Epiphanius didn't know about.

And, before you think that Alexander murdered Epiphanius and Johanna, rest assured that he did not. He certainly had a lot to gain from their death, but never planned on having them killed. In fact, he was doing quite well under their current, dishonest business relationship. However, between this morning when he first saw Nicholas and now this afternoon when he came to reassure him about the business, Alexander began to realize the massive opportunity that Nicholas's parents' death gave him.

"The gods must be in my favor," Alexander thought earlier that day. "Certainly, they are punishing Epiphanius for his foolish pursuit of Christianity." Alexander wasn't particularly religious, but he was never one to shy away from taking any advantage that any deity wanted to throw his way.

Alexander's mind swirled with the possibilities. Perhaps he could run the entire business himself. Nicholas was weak and young – it would be like stealing candy from a baby. And, while Alexander was heartfelt in his sadness for Nicholas, he was also beginning to concoct a plan of how to take the entire business, and its profits, for himself. Nicholas's grief, combined with his lack of experience, provided the perfect opportunity for Alexander.

"That's right, Nicholas. Don't worry about a thing. I will determine how much inventory we lost and I will make sure that we secure new materials to cover our current orders. You can trust me, Nicholas." With that, Alexander patted Nicholas on the back and told him he'd see him tomorrow at the service.

Not one to lose out on an opportunity to convert, Papa Antony decided he had everything he needed for the memorial service and hurried his wife out the door so they could walk with Alexander. They had about a quarter-mile walk in the same direction, so Papa Antony figured this would be a good opportunity to invite Alexander to church.

"I'll see you tomorrow, Nicholas," Papa Antony said. "Get plenty of rest and remember that God is still in control."

"Thank you, Papa Antony. I'll see you tomorrow."

Nicholas took great comfort in Alexander's kindness and the company of Aemilia and Rufus. He was confused and frustrated about God's role in this, but he was even comforted by the care of Papa Antony. Perhaps it was this first sense of calm since the morning's news that reminded Nicholas he was still thirsty from his time on the boat. Nicholas went to the cistern and took several deep drinks.

Faustina went home too and it was just Nicholas, Aemilia, and Rufus. They shared stories of Nicholas's parents and watched Nicholas swirl through emotions – laughing then crying then questioning God in anger, all to be repeated over and over throughout the evening.

They were three young adults trying to make sense of the confused world they lived in. Even in his grief, Nicholas led the conversation – that was who he was, a leader. True to her form, Aemilia comforted Nicholas. She badly wanted to rescue Nicholas from his pain and she kept reminding him that everything was going to be OK. And true to his form, Rufus was there in support. He was happy to be anywhere that Nicholas was – not quite yet a third wheel to Nicholas and Aemilia's growing relationship. Despite their strong personalities and character traits everything was going to turn upside down. It would soon be Rufus leading Nicholas, Nicholas rescuing Aemilia, and Aemilia losing hope and control. But let's not get ahead of ourselves.

After about an hour, it was getting late and Aemilia had to go home. Rufus offered to walk her home and then return back to stay the night with Nicholas so that Nicholas would not be alone heading into tomorrow's funeral. As Rufus walked Aemilia the short distance to her house, it started raining.

With Aemilia going home and Rufus temporarily gone, Nicholas was in the house alone – it was empty and quiet. Nicholas hardly ever stayed home by himself. He thought it was ironic – last night he sought to be alone on the sea, without a person in sight. Nicholas was trying to escape people and feel free to think by himself and be by himself. Now, tonight, he was alone in his own house and he wanted anything except to be alone. Thankfully Rufus was coming back.

Nicholas was angry at God. "This isn't a god I want to believe in," Nicholas fumed in his thoughts. "How could a good God take away my good parents. How could a good God send rain tonight but no rain when my parents were burning in the fire? How could a good God leave me all alone – no parents, no brothers, and no sisters?"

That night Nicholas tossed and turned, replaying the day's events over in his head. It continued to rain through the night, and sometime quite late, Nicholas finally fell asleep.

3 – Alexander

    Alexander was in his early fifties, medium height, and pretty skinny. A fairly perceptive person might look at him and automatically think there was something shady about his appearance – maybe it was the way he stood when no one was looking, kind of cocked to one side. Or, perhaps it was the way a smirky smile crept across his face when he thought of some devilish plan or idea. But, for the most part, people were drawn to Alexander. Like a great salesman, he had a way of charming his way into people's lives, making them feel like kings and queens – figuratively patting their backs with one hand while stealing their money with his other hand.
    Alexander lived in Myra his entire life. While that helped explain how he was so well connected throughout the region, it didn't explain his connections in far-off provinces. Those connections were courtesy of his father, Phillip.
    Ever since Alexander could remember, his father was a businessman. Not just any businessman – but one who tried to make money every way he could, even if it wasn't always honest. Alexander never understood his father's business practices as a boy, but as an adult, let's just say that the apple didn't fall far from the tree.

But, however good Phillip was at cheating customers and selling people things under false pretenses, he was completely opposite in his skill at being a father to Alexander. Alexander's earliest memories of his father were that of a drunken fool who didn't properly love his wife and wasn't too kind to Alexander.

"Alexander!" Phillip, likely drunk, yelled at Alexander when he was just 11 years old. "Why didn't you put the donkey away?!"

Alexander hated talking with his father when he had been drinking. He knew that he couldn't win, even if he did everything right.

"I did put her away, father."

"Curse you son! The donkey is out and it is going to rain. My good cloak is on that donkey and you are going to get it ruined!"

Nothing Philip said made any sense. The donkey was already put away and his father was wearing his good cloak.

"I'm sorry father. I'll go out right now and put her away," Alexander was sobbing. He knew he did nothing wrong, but he couldn't talk any sense into his father when he was like this. By this point in Alexander's life, his mother had already died of fever. He hated his father when he was drunk, but he respected him so much for his ability as a successful businessman. "When I'm older," he thought, "I will be a great businessman like my father – just not a drunk father to my children."

Now that Alexander was older, he could proudly claim that his boyhood proclamation proved true on both accounts. He was a great businessman and not a drunk father.

First, as for being a great businessman like his father... he got his deception honestly – remember the apple doesn't fall far from the tree.

Philip bought and sold anything he could to make a denarius. One day he met a man in Antioch who was selling worms – worms that looked unlike any type of worm Philip had ever seen. The man tried to convince Philip that they were silkworms and Philip believed him. Philip brought them back to

Myra where he intended to raise them to produce silk, which was very valuable.

Of course, we have the luxury of knowing history to know that silkworms didn't make their way to the west this early. So, as you might guess, Philip soon figured out that while his worms were unique, they weren't silkworms and didn't produce anything valuable at all.

Not to be outwitted and scammed himself, Philip decided to turn his deception into a profit. With the help of his 13-year old son, Alexander, Philip traveled all over Lycia selling the worms. A third century Harold Hill, he was always careful to sell just enough worms and stay just long enough in any given town before people found out he was a fraud. He had a few close calls – like the time he and Alexander dressed as women and snuck out of town – but he always got away. In the process, Alexander learned a lot from his father, and he learned that sometimes a dishonest denarius is easier to make than an honest denarius.

On the second count, not to be a drunk father to his children, Alexander accomplished that too – mainly because he never drank and he never had any children.

Now, not having any children – that is a bit of a sad story. It is curious to wonder what Alexander's life would have been like if his one true love would have worked out. Her name was Florentina and she lived in Alexandria, Egypt. Alexandria was always a frequent trip for Alexander – he probably had been there a dozen times before he met Florentina.

About ten years ago, Alexander visited Alexandria and met Florentina, who was the daughter of a prominent flax merchant. They immediately hit it off. In fact, for one of the only times in Alexander's life, he let something else take the place of his love of business. He even canceled sailing home with his flax shipment so that he could spend an extra month with Florentina (which, Alexander has never forgotten, cost him his extra share of the money he would have swindled away from Epiphanius).

Alexander knew it was true love, and Florentina did too. They spent much of their time together and began to make plans for Florentina to move to Myra. Pressed for time, they quickly threw together plans for a wedding. They were to be married and then on the next boat back to Myra within the month.

That was until Alexander tried to leave Alexandria with a bride *and* too good of a flax deal at the expense of his future father-in-law. Although he didn't necessarily want to cheat his future father-in-law by underpaying, he had already established a precedent for manipulating the ledger books from the last six shipments Alexander purchased from him. He knew that if he paid the full amount this time, Florentina's father would figure out that he hadn't been paying correctly every other time.

Well, suffice it to say, the sudden cost of the wedding had Florentina's father paying a little more attention to his money than he had before. He realized that Alexander cheated him in the past. Immediately the wedding was called off and Alexander had to choose between staying in town and likely going to jail, or escaping on the next boat and leaving Florentina behind. So much for true love.

It's OK to feel sorry for Alexander. His life might have been different if he married Florentina. His life might have been different if he had a different father. Instead, he decided to trust no one, not even his partner Epiphanius.

So, Alexander was a deceitful businessman. He was alone and he never married. But, there is one more event in Alexander's life that is important for Nicholas's story.

A few years after his failed relationship with Florentina, Alexander happened to meet Emperor Diocletian. Diocletian was emperor of the Roman Empire, though he chose to share his duties with Maximian. Diocletian was the father figure of the two rulers and, luckily for Alexander, focused his energy on the eastern half of the Roman Empire, where Myra was located.

Diocletian was often out securing Roman borders, but one fateful winter he was home in the de facto eastern capital, Nicomedia (which would later become Constantinople), which was the capital of the province of Bithynia. Alexander was in

Nicomedia securing trade deals and happened to be walking down a street when he heard two men arguing.

"You blaspheme our gods and our emperor!" one man yelled at another.

"I don't blaspheme anyone; however, my religion will not allow me to contribute an offering to your pagan festival," the second man replied.

"You aren't contributing to a pagan festival! You are contributing to Rome itself. Are you a Roman or not? The new law states that you must contribute. Do you defy the law?"

Not one to miss a good show, Alexander paused to listen to the argument. Diocletian had just passed laws that required all people, especially Christians, to contribute to Roman festivals. For most people, a Roman festival was a source of national pride – like a holiday. It actually had little to do with religion. However, many Christians saw the idolatry and immoral practices associated with the festival as acts of worshipping Roman gods. Therefore, many Christians refused to contribute, which was a punishable offense. Diocletian didn't like Christians (or at least he didn't like their morals), so he was happy to have them punished.

Moments later, Roman soldiers showed up to stop the argument. By this point both men were hollering at each other and the soldiers couldn't make sense of what was going on.

"You there! Did you witness this argument?" one of the soldiers directed the question toward Alexander.

"Yes… sir. I saw most of it," Alexander nervously reported.

"Well, out with it! What was going on here?"

With his response Alexander made a conscious decision. His answer was honest, but his motivation wasn't out of honesty. In the two seconds between the soldier's question and Alexander beginning to talk, Alexander realized that there might be some business to be made as a result of this newly rekindled Roman persecution of Christians.

"That man – he wasn't going to make the required contribution for the festival," Alexander spoke up, now with confidence. "I think it is abhorrent. And to show my support for Diocletian and all things Roman, this man's disobedience has inspired me to donate a double portion!"

With that statement, the Christian was arrested and Alexander found his 15 minutes of fame. The soldiers, who happened to rank high in the army, brought Alexander to the palace where Diocletian thanked him for his citizenship. As a token of his appreciation, Diocletian invited Alexander to that evening's feast and gave Alexander a small contract of wool for the Roman army. You would think that Alexander was smart enough to not cheat Diocletian, but Alexander didn't know how to conduct honest business. Luckily for Alexander, he got away with it for now.

Alexander was star struck by Diocletian – his power and his wealth. And, perhaps more than that, Alexander thirsted after the potentially large contracts he could get by supplying all of Diocletian's army with wool and linen. Alexander was not able to secure those contracts on this visit to Nicomedia, and it would be the only time he ever met Diocletian, but Alexander always thought about how he could get those contracts. He often lay awake at night, wondering what he could do to secure them. He remembered that his seemingly preordained encounter with Diocletian came because he witnessed against a Christian. While Emperor Diocletian was not fond of Christians, Alexander could care less for them or against them. His partner, however, was a Christian. So, Alexander decided to tell Epiphanius a different story about how he secured the emperor's wool contract and kept the Christian persecution part to himself. This experience with Diocletian is important – you will see that later.

*** *** *** *** *** *** *** *** *** *** ***

After leaving Nicholas's house and trying his best to endure his walk with Papa Antony, Alexander returned home to think about this sudden fortuitous turn of events. Alexander's plan to take complete control of the business from Nicholas was starting to form in his mind. It would take some time, but he was certain that he could accomplish it.

The problem is that this plan wasn't the only iron Alexander had in his scheming fire. Remember how Aemilia's parents, Stephen and Faustina, were losing pottery contracts and starting to have financial difficulties? That was Alexander's fault. Years ago, he partnered with Stephen to share a merchant ship's route from Myra to Corinth. Like usual, Alexander charged Stephen about 10% more than his share, except Stephen figured it out. Being a decent man, Stephen confronted Alexander privately, rather than publicly humiliate him. Alexander blew it off as a mistake, but grew very leery of Aemilia's family since that day. When the opportunity came to divert some pottery business away from them, Alexander jumped on it. He didn't even trade in pottery and he didn't even financially benefit from the deals he made to move business away from Aemilia's family. He did it anyway, just out of spite.

Alexander really didn't like Stephen – mainly because Stephen came close to exposing him. When Alexander saw Faustina cooking and helping Nicholas with the funeral preparations, his rage burned all the more intensely. While one side of his brain concocted a plan to take away the business from Nicholas, the other side of his brain searched for a plan to get back at Stephen for good.

Alexander was trying to go to sleep that night when the worst idea hit him all at once. It's fascinating how a person's most ingenious ideas or most difficult solutions explode into ones head in the stillness of quiet. In a moment of stunning clarity, it seemed Alexander had a plan to get back at Aemilia's family. It was like the plan formed in an instant and in the same instant Alexander understood fully what he was going to do.

He knew they were having trouble financially and would likely lose their house and possessions. But, that wasn't good enough. Alexander realized that Aemilia's parents had something more precious to lose – their very daughters.

Now we've already established that Alexander wasn't a murderer, though it's possible that murder might have been a more humane plan of revenge. Instead, Alexander saw a clear path toward slavery – a devilishly easy way for Aemilia's parents to lose all three daughters to a fate worse than death – to be sold as slaves and to belong to another person.

Taking a play out his old playbook, Alexander knew that all he had to do was accuse Aemilia's family of violating Emperor Diocletian's edicts to support Rome in every way. The penalty was quite steep financially, and Roman law allowed that if one couldn't pay a fine, then his children were to be sold as slaves. Furthermore, other people could not pay the fine on your behalf or else they would appear to be taking part in your guilty treason. Nicholas, or anyone else for that matter, would not be able to pay Aemilia's father's fine. Which it didn't matter, because Alexander was plotting to take all of Nicholas's money anyway when he took away Nicholas's share of the business.

So, in one single day, Alexander came up with two evil schemes. One scheme was to take Nicholas's money and his share of the business. The second scheme was to take Stephen's daughters. A slight smile crept across Alexander's face as he lay in bed. "How did I ever become so evil," he thought, letting out a laugh that even his neighbors could hear. "Oh yeah. Thanks Dad!"

4 – The Barn

Nicholas woke up the day after the funeral feeling a little better. Yesterday was such a blur – family and friends all packed into the small church. Then there was the dinner at Aemilia's home. Nicholas was relieved the day was over and today he was determined to go to the barn.

As promised, Aemilia came to Nicholas's house early in the morning. They got Nicholas's horse and his father's wagon and took off toward the barn. Riding with Nicholas on the wagon reminded her of a day, earlier this summer, when Nicholas took her out on his boat. Their parents were OK with it. After all, Nicholas was experienced on the sea and both sets of parents trusted them to be together. In fact, both sets of parents encouraged Nicholas and Aemilia's friendship. Nicholas's parents and Aemilia's parents had both found true love, and they hoped Nicholas and Aemilia might have a chance at that too.

That day when they were on the sea, the sky was so free of clouds that it was difficult to tell where the sea ended and the sky began. It's often in a state of such grandeur when we ourselves feel small and begin to ponder the big questions of life.

"Nicholas, do you really believe that God created all of this?"

"I can't really think of any other way to explain it, Aemilia."

"Do you think God knows about each and every fish in this water? When someone catches a fish, does God know one less is there?"

"The scripture says that God knows every hair on your head, so I suppose it's not a big thing for him to know how many fish are in the water."

"Yeah, but all over the earth, people are catching fish and new ones hatch. Do you think that God just keeps a running tally in his head? Wouldn't that number always change?"

"Aemilia, you're asking some pretty crazy questions. I don't know… I guess God just knows. He is God. I think that kind of knowledge just goes with the territory."

You see, we are getting to know Nicholas during a dark time of his life when his faith was shaky and his outlook was bleak. However, Nicholas had an upbringing of a solid foundation of faith in God, though that foundation was surely being tested now. It's while we are in the storm that our perspective is skewed and our vision is clouded. In a literal storm, you might not be able to see 50 feet in front of you, but on a clear day you can see for miles. With the death of his parents, Nicholas was in a storm, only seeing the wind-driven rain of sorrow and tears. Nicholas was forgetting the miles-long view of faith and perspective he previously had just months before his parents' death.

The barn was about a 30-minute walk from Nicholas's house. With the horse and cart, it was about a 15-minute ride. Being wealthy, Nicholas's family had one horse. Aemilia's family used to have a horse, but recently sold it. Rufus's family didn't have money for a horse or even a donkey.

Nicholas never quite understood why his father's barns had to be so far from home. The truth was that Nicholas's home was in a neighborhood of wealthy homes in Myra – wealthy for the late third century. In his neighborhood alone, there were three men on the town council, a retired military general, and about a dozen rich businessmen. While Aemilia's home wasn't in Nicholas's neighborhood, it was in another wealthy neighborhood, still in the rich part of town.

Between Nicholas's house and the barn was the center of Myra itself. Myra was a quickly growing city – both in size and importance. Its main area had a newly constructed bathhouse, various temples, government buildings, and a large marketplace. The crown jewel, however, was Myra's amphitheater. A combination of Greek and Roman architecture, the amphitheater had nearly 40 rows of seats and could host over 10,000 spectators. It was nestled right up against the side of large cliffs, cliffs that would later house famous carved tombs that still exist today.

Alexander lived near the center of town – he felt like he had to have his social hand in a little bit of everything. So, he lived not too far from the wealthy neighborhoods, not too far from the bay, and definitely not too far from the government buildings and marketplace.

The barn, however, was not in the wealthy part of Myra. For one, it wouldn't make much sense to use valuable land to construct something as inconsequential as a barn. For two, the barn was close to the bay and therefore convenient for loading and unloading materials. Being close to the bay was great for barns and sailors, but not quite a desirable place to live. While the homes, or rather apartments, around the barn were filled with generally good and honest people, they weren't very well-off financially. Many of the area families had fathers who sailed and were gone at sea for months at a time. Most families near the barn barely scraped by – working hard, but not always having a lot to show for their work. This is the neighborhood that Rufus lived in.

Myra's bay had two large statues marking its entrance from the sea – one for Emperor Germanicus (a well-respected Roman leader) and the other for his wife Agrippina. Myra wasn't just home to textile and pottery businesses, it was also home to large grain businesses. Ships from Egypt would often cross straight north through the Mediterranean Sea and use Myra as a distribution hub to a large part of the Roman Empire. In fact, Emperor Hadrian built a large grain warehouse near the harbor – a structure that still exists in some form today.

    Nicholas and Aemilia rode nearly the entire distance to the barn in silence. Along the way, they passed a crippled man on the street, begging for food or money. This was actually the same beggar who Nicholas ran past earlier two mornings ago, when he was trying desperately to get to church on time. It was common during this period that people who were disabled or diseased were left to fend for themselves, depending on the generosity of others. Nicholas glanced at the man and had no compassion. "His week can't be worse than mine," he thought. In fact, Nicholas started feeling angry about the man. "Where is his god?" he actually said out loud, motioning toward the man as they rode by, "Take up thy bed and walk." Nicholas wasn't normally heartless in such matters, just perhaps a little numb today.

    Aemilia tossed the beggar a coin. She looked at Nicholas with a little bit of disbelief, though he didn't see it. "How could his heart be so cold?" she wondered, while acknowledging that she had never experienced anything like Nicholas was experiencing. Aemilia was never one for a small heart – she always had compassion, even when it wasn't much deserved. In fact, she often carried spare change just in case of encounters like this one.

    The burnt barn, now almost in sight, was a large wooden structure with two levels. The first level contained a small reception area where employees would record the movement of wool and linen in and out of its doors. There was a large dyeing room on the main floor where employees would give vibrant color to the material before it was shipped on to its next destination. Nicholas learned from his father that dyeing the material made it much more valuable, especially dyeing it with purple dye. Purple dye was very expensive, however, and only a small amount of wool and linen was ever dyed purple.

Aside from the reception area and dyeing room, there were also rooms that stored the dyes and stored some linen on the first floor. Most wool and linen, however, were stored on the large, open second floor. When he was a boy, Nicholas loved playing in between the stacks of material on the second floor. He and his friends would play hide and seek, play army, or hide from his dad when his dad was ready to go home.

Rufus met Nicholas and Amelia a couple of blocks away from the barn, where his road intersected with the road Nicholas and Aemilia were traveling.

"Wow, I can't believe it is still smoking," Nicholas said with unbelief as they saw the remains of the barn sitting at the end of the street.

"Yeah, but there was a lot more smoke when I stopped by a couple of days ago," Rufus shared, always happy when he knew information that other people didn't know. He wasn't always the smartest or full of a lot of facts, so he felt an extra bit of pride when he could display his knowledge.

"There's just nothing left, Nick," said Aemilia, for the first time reacting with her speech instead of thinking about how it might affect Nicholas. "Oh, I'm sorry. That wasn't a very nice thing to say."

"It's OK. It's true," said Nicholas gruffly. Aemilia was already starting to cry – overcome with grief for her friend and embarrassment that she let down her guard. Nicholas wasn't crying, however. He just sat there in disbelief.

Getting off of the cart, Nicholas began to think about what was in the barn. "There must have been hundreds of amorphas of linen alone, not counting all of the wool," Nicholas said in mild shock. (One amorpha was about a dozen bundles of linen stacked together.)

Then, Nicholas quickly realized he was talking of burned up linen and wool, when the same fire took his parents' lives. "What were they thinking? Why would they try to put it out?

How could they try to put it out?" he began saying out loud the questions that kept running through his head.

Rufus, remembering he had more information to share, replied, "When I stopped by on Sunday, some men said the flames looked like they reached the clouds. One man said he saw your parents run into the barn when only the back of the barn was on fire. He said less than a minute later the entire thing collapsed and made the most terrible sound. He said he and others tried to get to your parents, but the flames were too intense." Then, realizing that he was taking a little too much pride in sharing his information without regarding his friend's situation, he stopped talking.

Nicholas stood at the former entrance to the barn, quiet and sullen. His friends felt awkward standing there with him, but didn't want to speak.

"My parents had more than just linen and wool in this barn," Nicholas began to whisper. "My father also kept most of our family's coins here. In fact, he liked to keep very little money at the house. He figured having a lot of money around would make it unsafe for mom and me – that it would invite robbers and such."

"Your entire family's fortune is here?" Rufus asked, returning to his normal place of student instead of teacher. "What if it's all melted?"

"It would take way more heat than from a bunch of lit-up linen to melt those coins," Nicholas replied. "He kept the money in the middle of the barn, so I suppose it should be buried in the pile about over there."

It's important to understand that Nicholas's family was quite wealthy. Nicholas's father kept a little bit of money at the house, but most of it at the barn. He didn't really use banks – only a small amount of money was kept on hold by local argentarii, Roman bankers who helped facilitate currency conversions when trading.

"I know money is important, but even more important is my great-grandfather's gold necklace. My father kept it here with the money for safekeeping. It has been passed down from father to father to father for over 70 years. I really want to find that necklace."

While it is true that Epiphanius was not born a rich man, he always had the family's gold necklace. It wasn't necessarily worth a lot of money, but it was very sentimental to him and, for the first time, apparently sentimental to Nicholas as well. The necklace was one of a kind and custom made for Nicholas's great-grandfather.

The necklace contained a chi rho symbol with a circle around it, and three wavy lines cutting across the middle. All of this was molded as a single image and attached to a gold chain.

Epiphanius's grandfather had the necklace made when he converted to Christianity. At the time, converting to Christianity was risky. He made the necklace to wear as a reminder to himself of his faith. To him, the three emblems reminded him of the Trinity – chi and rho (the first two Greek letters of "Christ") for representing Jesus, the circle for representing the omniscience of the Father, and the wavy lines for the Holy Spirit. Just before Nicholas's grandfather (Epiphanius's father) passed away, he gave Epiphanius the necklace to wear. Epiphanius hardly wore it however, choosing instead to keep it safe in the linen barn with the family's coins.

It's interesting that Nicholas was more concerned about the necklace than the money. It's not that Nicholas didn't value money – though he had too little of an understanding of how difficult his life would be without his parents' money. Instead, it's interesting that Nicholas remembered the necklace at all. His father rarely spoke of it and Nicholas never really knew his grandfather, let alone his great-grandfather. It's funny how death can suddenly change one's perspective on what is important and valuable. Suddenly heirlooms remind us of those we've lost and are irreplaceable when the heirlooms themselves are lost.

Nicholas and Aemilia brought the cart because he intended on getting his father's money and the necklace. The sun was bright – there was no rain in sight. They had a lot of work ahead of them, and it actually began to invigorate Nicholas to have such a task to accomplish. After all, if he couldn't find his family's wealth, then he would likely have to sell off much of what he had. And, while the necklace wasn't worth much money, he really wanted to find it too.

Some of his father's employees were at the barn, sifting through wreckage in the back, trying to salvage any wool or linen that might have survived the fire. When Nicholas arrived, he thanked them for their help and asked them to leave him to be alone with his friends. They were considerate of Nicholas's feelings, wondering themselves how the death of his parents would affect their jobs. They left, agreeing with Nicholas that they would return tomorrow to continue their salvaging effort.

"My father showed me once where he kept the money in the barn," Nicholas proclaimed to his two friends. "He had three holes made into the floor, right over there where the middle of the barn was. He kept the money in bags in those holes in the ground."

"Well, let's get to work," Rufus responded.

So, the three of them began picking through the ruble to get to the middle of the barn. It was a big mess – not just burned wood, linen, and wool from the fire, but also wet wood, wet linen, and wet wool from the rain two nights ago. They worked hard, but were careful when moving large, partially burned pieces of wood that might make other pieces shift or fall.

"Be careful, Nick!" Aemilia hollered as a beam shifted and sent some wood crashing down. It really wasn't that big of a deal, but she was concerned nevertheless.

After about an hour, they made it to where Nicholas thought the three holes should be. It took another half hour to clear enough debris so that they were confidently at ground level.

"There, I'm pretty sure that's one of them," Nicholas stated. "See that charred wood on the ground? That's a cover to one of the holes."

Quickly and more carelessly moving debris away, they unmasked the entire wood covering of the hole. Now, when I say hole, it was more like a little storage room. It wasn't quite big enough to be called a room, but it was deep enough that a person typically needed help to get down into it and you could stretch your arms in each direction while just barely hitting the sides of the hole.

Removing the cover, Nicholas hopped down into the hole without any assistance. The sun was bright, and with the wood cover mostly covering the hole during the fire, its contents were clean and arranged as his father left them.

Nicholas lifted up seven heavy bags of coins. "Unbelievable!" exclaimed Rufus. "There's more money in one of these bags than I've had my entire life!" Rufus was right. Each bag contained enough money for Nicholas to live comfortably for a third of his life. Despite Alexander's efforts to cheat Nicholas's parents, they still made a lot of money.

"That's all that's down here," Nicholas declared. I don't see the necklace."

"Would it be in one of the bags?" Aemilia asked.

"No, my father kept it in a wood box. It isn't here; it must be in one of the other two holes."

Rufus extended a hand to Nicholas and helped Nicholas get out of the first storage hole. They immediately began looking for the second hole and found it pretty quickly.

About ten minutes later with the hole uncovered, Nicholas hopped down and discovered eight more bags of coins and a scroll.

Nicholas looked at the scroll – it was full of numbers. It read…

3 * 8 * 1 * 19 * 5 * 4
15-4 * 33-3 * 48-6 * 15-9
62-6 * 53-3 * 46-7 * 23-4 * 22-4
21-8 * 29-4 * 48-6 * 34-8
59-5 * 37-4 * 28-54 * 33-3 * 58-4 * 33-3

Nicholas couldn't make sense of it. He figured that it had something to do with his father's inventory or money. Regardless, he handed the scroll up to Rufus with the bags of money and was disappointed not to find the necklace.

"It's OK, Nick," Aemilia comforted. "The necklace has to be in the third hole."

"I sure hope so," responded Nicholas. "Believe me, I know the money is important, but that necklace means so much to me right now."

The group found the third hole pretty quickly. In fact, it's a wonder that they didn't find this hole first because it was fairly clear of debris.

"Wow, Nick, this hole is going to be easy to get to. There's hardly anything on top of it!" Aemilia exclaimed, always trying to find the bright side in any negative situation.

"Let's hope so," Rufus chimed in.

"Well, let's find out," Nicholas replied.

With that, they reached down toward the cover, brushed aside a little bit of ash, and quickly uncovered the wooden lid to the hole.

"Here goes nothing" Nicholas spoke as he picked up the wood cover and flung it to the side, almost hitting Aemilia in the process. Nicholas jumped down into the hole.

"What is it, Nick? Do you see the necklace?" Aemilia asked, with a voice that was part-encouraging and part-worried.

Nicholas didn't respond.

"Do you need help lifting things out, Nick?" Rufus added, with a double-shot of optimism in his voice.

Nicholas still didn't respond.

Slightly out of character, Aemilia jumped down into the hole. It was fairly dark, but still bright enough to see around. The walls were mostly dirt with some vertical beams serving as supports on the sides. There was actually a wood floor, the most room-like part of the entire hole. Doing a slow turn around the hole, Aemilia saw a couple of empty shelves on one side, a couple of loose coins on the ground, and nothing else except

Nicholas sitting on the floor crying, holding a dirty brownish, red coat.

Aemilia took a step over to Nicholas, placed her hand on his shoulder, and said "I'm so sorry, Nick."

Rufus peeked his head down into the hole, and with a little less compassion than would have been nice, exclaimed, "It's all gone!"

Nicholas felt like he was being kicked when he was already down. Sure, he had 15 bags of coins and that was more than he would ever need in life. Sure, he had two great friends and the loving support of his community at yesterday's memorial service. But all Nicholas really wanted right now was that necklace – a reminder of his dad and a reminder of who he was.

It's kind of funny, actually, that the missing necklace was a Christian symbol. As Nicholas sat in that hole, trying to sniff back tears, his mind began to fill with thoughts of abandoning his faith. "My faith is gone, like that necklace," Nicholas thought, this time making sure the words weren't actually coming out of his mouth. "Where is God in any of this?"

"So, what's that coat, Nick? Why was it in the hole?" Rufus asked, interrupting Nicholas's thoughts about the necklace.

"This coat belonged to my dad. He used to wear it when he was working in the barn whenever it was a little cold outside."

"It looks like it used to be a nice coat," Aemilia chimed in, trying to lift Nicholas's mood.

"The coat has a bit of a story. My dad had an order to dye a handful of coats purple – for some rich guy all the way in Rome. Alexander brought these coats from Dacia. Purple is an expensive dye, and my dad was trying to get the dye just right – it was one of his first times mixing purple. Well, he tried it on the first coat, and you can see what happened. He ruined this one, but fortunately figured it out for the other coats. Anyway, since this one was ruined and a weird, bright red color, he decided to wear it around the barn when he was cold. It's definitely not red anymore – too many years of dirt and hard work have made it kind of brown."

"Come to think of it, I think I've seen him wearing that before," Rufus said, remembering Nicholas's dad wearing the coat when Epiphanius jumped in and help Rufus's dad while loading linen a few times.

"Well, it's not the necklace. Where could that thing be? And why is this room empty of coins?" Nicholas asked, thinking out loud.

"Since your dad's coat was down there, maybe he was working in there," Aemilia offered. "Maybe he moved the money to somewhere else."

"Who knows," Nicholas said dejected. "Hopefully it's not stolen. I'll probably never figure it out." With that said, Nicholas threw down the coat.

The trio spent the next half hour loading up the bags of coins and scrolls. They found a couple of barely preserved ledger papers in the reception area and loaded up those as well. When Nicholas was preoccupied looking at the ledger papers, Aemilia went back to the third hole, picked up the coat, and loaded it too. They didn't talk much while working – Nicholas was deeply grateful for his friends' help, but he was also deeply hurt that the necklace wasn't there.

Finally, when they were about finished, Aemilia spoke up – breaking the near half-hour silence. "Maybe your dad kept the necklace somewhere else, Nick."

"Maybe, but probably not." Nicholas wasn't in much of a mood for optimism.

"Do you think one of the workers took it?" Rufus asked.

"Rufus, I've known those guys my entire life. They've been like uncles and cousins to me. There's no way they took the money or the necklace."

"Yeah, I suppose you're right," Rufus agreed in words but not in thought. His upbringing taught him that just about anybody would do something wrong in the right circumstances. His father didn't trust too many people and Rufus didn't have the Christian perspective of believing the best in people. In fact, other than the times that Nicholas took his friend to church, Rufus never stepped foot inside of one.

With the wagon loaded, Nicholas and Aemilia told Rufus goodbye and drove the wagon to Nicholas's house. They had quite a bit of money with them, so they were careful to cover the bags with the oldest looking blankets they could find – ones they brought earlier from Nicholas's home. Actually, Nicholas's worst-looking blankets were still better than most people's best blankets, but it did the trick. No one bothered them their entire way home and they unloaded the contents into Nicholas's house.

"Why don't you let me stay and make us some lunch?" Aemilia asked.

"No, that's OK. I'm not really hungry." Nicholas was being mostly true, but he was really just wanting to spend some time alone.

"Come on, Nick, I don't mind."

"No, really Aemilia. I appreciate it, but I think I'd like to rest here alone." He wasn't trying to deceive her, but he actually planned to look through some of his parents' stuff. He really didn't want to say that though, and he also just wanted to be alone.

"OK, if that's what you want." It wasn't what Aemilia wanted and she was pretty sure it wasn't what Nicholas needed, but she gave in anyway. "I'll see you later, Nick." Of course, they didn't have plans to see each other later – most of the time they saw each other by "chance" when one of them was going somewhere or at a family party or community event.

"Bye, Aemilia. Thanks for your help."

"Sure, Nick. Let me know if you need anything, anything at all. Even if you just want to sit around and cry." That last part didn't quite come out how she meant it, and Nicholas didn't make a big deal of it. Aemilia left and Nicholas sat in his big, empty house – a house that seemed much lonelier than ever before, much colder than ever before, and much emptier than ever before.

That afternoon was not a good afternoon for Nicholas to be alone. The rest of the day, Nicholas was tormented with an avalanche of thoughts, yet no thought seemed to last long enough to really think it through.

"Where is that necklace?"

"Why does the stupid necklace even matter to me?"

"Does God even exist?"

"Maybe all gods are the same, if there are any at all."

"Papa Antony thinks I could be a priest? Hah! I'm not sure God even cares."

"Why are my parents gone?"

"Where are my parents? Is there really a heaven?"

"If there's not a heaven, then are they anywhere? Is it good? Is it bad? Can I ever see them?"

"I can't run the business."

"Alexander is going to think I'm a fool. I'm going to lose all of our money."

"I can't live in this house alone."

"I bet Neptune is going to die next."

All afternoon and evening, Nicholas wrestled in his own mind. He couldn't find any peace, and the darkness that slowly enveloped the outside of the house as evening wore on mirrored the darkness that slowly enveloped his soul.

Finally, Nicholas fell asleep.

5 – Jailed

The summer's warmth gave way to autumn's chill. The mountain leaves lost their will for life and stumbled to the ground. The sea forgot its summer calm and surrendered to winter's waves. Nicholas's empty days stretched into weeks and then into months.

The next three months were a dark time for Nicholas. He was such a pleasant, optimistic young man, but not during this time. Nicholas didn't go to church. He barely talked to Aemilia. Rufus kept trying to get Nicholas to fish or to sail or to do anything, but he wouldn't.

In what should have been a time of meeting with his father's employees and business partners, Nicholas instead stayed locked inside his house. He barely thought anything about the business. When he did, he reasoned that Alexander was taking care of it like he said he would.

Nicholas's faith was all but extinct. Whereas he spent his first several days after his parents' death questioning God, now he felt like even that was a waste of time. "Why question something that doesn't seem to exist?" Nicholas said to himself at least once each day.

It was kind of odd, actually, but Nicholas was obsessed with the decision that he made daily to forsake God. From the outside looking in, it is obvious that Nicholas was just trying to convince himself of his perceived apostasy. The simple fact that he continually dwelled on it was proof that he wasn't quite willing to let go of God.

As for Aemilia, she tried to see Nicholas, but it hurt her so much to see him like this. As much as she wanted to be a healer and to love him through his hurt, his apathy toward her struck her soul in a way that cut her deeply. In fact, if there was any way to make Aemilia feel unloved, then Nicholas's complete disregard for her care was that one way. She cried every night for Nicholas, crying in prayer, crying in talks with her mom, and crying in her sleep. She couldn't understand how someone with such light and love as Nicholas could be as dark and cold as he had become. For her own health, she began limiting her visits. At first, she skipped a day or two a week. Then she skipped two days in a row. Finally, after three months, she found herself realizing that she hadn't seen Nicholas in over a week.

Rufus, much like a trusted dog, never gave up on trying to see Nicholas. He stopped by every day, unfazed by Nicholas's lack of care or response. Though he didn't have much money or food himself, he often brought Nicholas leftover bread or some fish that he had caught earlier that evening. Rufus optimistically asked Nicholas to join him on some quest or adventure, but Nicholas always refused. Despite Nicholas's often-curt responses, Rufus never lost hope or optimism that Nicholas would come around.

*** *** *** *** *** *** *** *** *** *** ***

During the three months that Nicholas grieved and spiraled deeper into his misery, Alexander was not only busy plotting his takeover of the business and his plan to take Nicholas's money, but he was also busy planning his revenge against Stephen and Faustina. He spent the three months not only fine-tuning his plan, but also working overtime trying to take away business from Stephen and severing Stephen's business relationships with local merchants.

"Since when did you get into the pottery business?" Titus asked Alexander.

"Well, Titus, like you, I am a man who likes to make a denarius any way I can," Alexander replied.

Titus had been trading with Alexander in textiles for about a dozen years. Working in the nearby province of Cilicia, Titus traded in whatever he could make money – textiles, pottery, leather, lead, spices, and more.

"Well, I've always worked with a guy named Stephen when it comes to pottery. You might know him, actually. I think he lives in Myra like you."

"Stephen, Stephen, Stephen…," Alexander was acting like he wasn't sure who Stephen was, then feigned his sudden realization. "Oh yeah, I know Stephen. Now listen," Alexander leaned in and spoke softer, "I shouldn't tell you this, but I don't think Stephen is a good long-term business partner for you."

"Oh yeah, and why not?"

"Rumor has it – actually it is stronger than a rumor, I know it to be true, but I can't tell you how… Rumor has it that Stephen is in all kinds of trouble. You hear things about him cheating merchants from Macedonia to Syria. Now, I don't know about that, but I do know that the local magistrate is opening an investigation into tax fraud."

"You don't say…" Titus didn't really care about Stephen's problems, but was always interested in juicy gossip.

"Yes, I'm afraid it's true. I would just hate for you to find yourself having paid Stephen for something that he couldn't deliver. It is hard to deliver pottery when you're in jail, you know."

Titus and Alexander chuckled. Titus slapped Alexander on the back and said, "And of course, it doesn't hurt that good old Alexander is here to save the day. I am so *lucky*…," Titus emphasized, "lucky that *you* can provide the pottery that I need to sell."

"You know me Titus, I'm here to serve," Alexander sneered while he talked. Alexander was always careful to charm his associates, but he knew that he and Titus were cut from the same deceptive cloth and Titus probably suspected that Alexander was up to no good.

"OK, then," Titus surmised. "It is settled, I will buy my pottery from you and not from Stephen. Now, where do you plan to get your pottery that I'm going to buy?"

"Don't you worry about that, Titus. I'll have it for you."

With another slap on the back and a hearty handshake, Alexander successfully steered another merchant away from Stephen. He hadn't really created a plan how he was going to supply all of this pottery that he promised while travelling from town to town, but he figured with Stephen's business soon out of the way he could simply step right in and take over Stephen's supply.

When you think about Alexander, don't be confused by his desire to deceive and make a dishonest denarius and wrongly think that he was lazy and against hard work. In fact, Alexander was anything but lazy. All of his lies and deceits took a lot of work. In some respects, Alexander could have made as much or more money by expending his energy in positive, wholesome pursuits, but it wouldn't have given him as much joy – as corrupted as that sounds.

Alexander was taking Stephen's business and now it was time to take his girls. With all of his secret pottery deals in place, Alexander secretly brought charges against Stephen and Faustina before Myra's magistrate – and the rest of his plan was set into motion.

Knock, Knock! Knock, Knock! The knocks were loud and deliberate. Stephen couldn't imagine who it could be – it was early in the morning and quite unusual to have guests so early. Stephen was already awake, going over his struggling business's financials. As he opened the door, Faustina came out of the bedroom, wandering what the commotion was about.

"Stephen of Myra, owner of pottery businesses and follower of the Christian religion, I have an order for your arrest," declared a soldier who was standing at his door.

"Arrest?" Stephen exclaimed loudly, sure to wake up his daughters.

"Arrest? What's this about?" Faustina was even louder in her disbelief, sure to wake up the neighbors.

"You are found to be in violation of the edict of the great Emperor Diocletian that requires all Roman citizens to act like Roman citizens – you must celebrate Roman holidays, pay Roman taxes, and obey Roman laws. You are a Roman, but do not live as a Roman. Therefore, you are under arrest."

"This is absurd! I haven't disobeyed any laws! I pay my taxes. I do everything I'm supposed to do."

"Arrest him!" With that command, a couple of soldiers bound Stephen and hurried him out of the house and onto a cart. Faustina ran outside after him, but was ordered to stop.

In the commotion all three girls emerged from their bedrooms, half asleep and fully confused.

"What's this about? Where are you taking my father?" Iris screamed, chasing the soldiers who already had Stephen out the door and hurrying down the street.

Faustina, herself overwhelmed by the sudden events, stopped Iris and pulled her inside, shutting the door.

"They say your father has violated the law." Faustina said, doing her best to understand what just happened.

"What laws?" Diantha asked.

"For not being a good enough Roman," Faustina replied.

"For being a Christian," Aemilia countered. "They arrested our father because he is a Christian. I've heard that they might start doing that! It is so wrong!"

"That's not right!" Iris started defiantly, then softened her speech as her confidence waned. "They can't do that, can they? Mother, they can't do that, can they?"

By now, Faustina was numb and softly crying and didn't hear Iris's question.

"Mother! They can't do that can they?" Iris asked, louder and with a little bit of renewed defiance.

"I don't know, Iris," Faustina replied. "These days, I don't hardly know which way is up."

The soldiers took Stephen to jail and placed him in a cell. A few hours later they brought him before the town magistrate who outlined the charges against Stephen. He was charged with subverting the Roman government by failing to supply his portion of animals for sacrifice during the festival to Faunus – a Roman god of the woodlands, fields and flock fertility. Diocletian's edict required wealthy merchants to supply animals for sacrifice for this and other festivals. It hadn't been enforced yet, and Alexander saw it as a great opportunity to get Stephen in trouble. Of course, providing sacrificial animals for such pagan festivals flew in the face of Stephen's Christianity. While some Christians justified their donations as "rendering to Caesar what is Caesar's" or as simply supporting a local festival, Stephen was convicted by his faith that he shouldn't participate. Furthermore, his recent financial struggles made it nearly impossible for him to finance the required donation of five calves.

Alexander knew that Stephen hadn't provided the animals, just like Stephen and many other wealthy Christians had refused to do for several years. So, with Diocletian's renewed focus on forcing Christians to participate or pay the price, Alexander decided that he could easily get Stephen in trouble. For that matter, he could have probably gotten at least a dozen other wealthy Myran Christians in trouble, but that wasn't his concern. Though, I'm sure if he gave it more thought, he could have found a way to extort money from them as well.

"The fine for your crime against Rome is 15,000 denarii – payable immediately," the magistrate decreed.

"15,000 denarii! That's insane! That is way more money than the five calves would have cost. How does this punishment fit the crime?"

"The price is 15,000 denarii by edict of Emperor Diocletian. You have to pay today or we take your home." With that said, the magistrate ordered Stephen to be taken out of the room.

You might think that Stephen paying 15,000 denarii or losing his house would have been sweet revenge to Alexander. After all, his complaint against Stephen was only that Stephen had discovered his dishonesty and privately called him out. Stephen could have certainly humiliated Alexander publicly, but he didn't. In truth, Stephen handled his previous discovery of Alexander's dishonesty in the best possible way for Alexander. That didn't matter to Alexander, however.

Alexander had bigger plans than taking Stephen's money or home. His plan was pretty convoluted, displaying the true darkness that his life full of deceit had created. It actually would have been much easier and certainly a surer punishment to let Stephen's trouble end at either the fine or losing the house, but Alexander desired something far worse.

Alexander's plan was simple and it went off without a hitch.

First, he swooped in and saved the day by loaning Stephen the 15,000 denarii. Although loaning the money was illegal, Alexander had already taken care of that. Unbeknownst to Stephen, Alexander attended the court procedure that day, staying in the back of the room, off to the side where he couldn't easily be seen. The magistrate was his close friend (more like occasional partner in crime) and the magistrate allowed Alexander to visit Stephen in his jail cell.

"Stephen, I just couldn't believe it when I heard the news. What is this country coming to?"

"Alexander, what on earth are you doing here?"

"I was shocked that someone who runs circles such as ours could find himself in a situation like this. Absolutely shocked."

Of course, Stephen didn't trust Alexander, especially since their incident a few years earlier. But, they still saw each other at plenty of festivals and parties. Stephen determined to always be cordial to Alexander and extend to him the benefit of the doubt, hoping that his former deceit was a one-time thing and that he was a changed man.

"Well, Alexander, this is what times have come to. Diocletian really has it in for Christians." Stephen let go of his surprise that Alexander was there.

Alexander could sense the change in tone in Stephen's voice and really began to turn on his charm. That is something he was very good at – charming his way into people's hearts.

"It is just wrong, Stephen, absolutely wrong. I'm so sorry – I wish there is something I could do."

Then, utilizing his acting skills that he would use again on Nicholas in the coming week, Alexander placed his arm on Stephen's shoulder and even conjured up tears in his eyes.

"Wait a second," Alexander whispered optimistically. "Why don't I loan you the money? It's not really a big deal – I could have it by this afternoon." Of course, he already had the money ready.

"Oh Alexander, I don't know if I could take it from you. I don't even know if I could pay it back," Stephen paused, thinking about it for a moment. "Besides, isn't it against the law? You can't help me or you'll be liable too."

"Well, well. Let's just say that the magistrate is a friend of mine and I'm certain he would look the other way. He's just doing his job – he certainly doesn't want someone like one of us to be thrown into jail – what a humiliation that would be to the upper class. As for paying me back, certainly you could – and we could work out those details later. Let me do it for you. I just couldn't imagine your family losing your home. And, if you don't have the money today, then that is exactly what will happen."

"I don't know Alexander."

"Come on. Let me do it... as a friend."

"Well, I suppose I could sell a few contracts and pay you back in a week. I really don't want it to drag out longer than that."

"A week?!" Alexander acted shocked by the short time period, but was inwardly ecstatic that Stephen was acting so rashly. "Do you think you could get it so soon?"

"Yes, only one week," Stephen replied. He was fully stubborn and fiercely independent.

"Perfect! I will go get the money and draw a simple contract – you know, just to keep things on the up and up. I'll be back in a few hours with the money and the contract and you will be out of here in no time."

Alexander bound out of the cell and Stephen sat there dumbfounded – absolutely flabbergasted that Alexander would help him and a little worried that he and Alexander might get in trouble because Alexander was loaning him the money. He kind of felt like he might be making a deal with the Devil. He thought that Alexander must be up to something, but immediately chastised himself for doubting someone who was being so nice to help.

Alexander did show up a couple of hours later as promised. He had the money and a contract. It was a simple contract, but very tightly crafted. Stephen would have one week to repay Alexander – that might seem a little harsh, but remember, it was actually the terms that Stephen wanted. He was a proud man and had a lot of trouble accepting help from another person. Besides, he knew he had several contracts he could sell in a short time and repay Alexander.

So, they signed the contract, Alexander paid the magistrate the money (and a little extra to keep him quiet), and Stephen was on his way home.

The next week was very difficult for Stephen and his family. Trying as hard as he could, he could not sell his contracts – hardly a single one. It was as if every businessman in Myra and beyond was working against him. (Thanks to Alexander, they were.) Stephen finally unloaded one contract, worth 1,500 denarii, but he couldn't sell any more during the week. Of course, it wasn't by chance that he couldn't sell his contracts – Alexander had been working very hard for not just this week, but for the last few months. He bribed and blackmailed and promised and did anything else he could do with the local merchants to keep them from working with Stephen. Alexander had a way of knowing the worst about people, and he used that knowledge to get them to do what he wanted. It's kind of ironic how much time and money Alexander spent working against Stephen. It was a good thing that he planned to take all of Nicholas's money soon or else Alexander might have gone bankrupt.

Speaking of Nicholas, he had no idea what was going on with Aemilia's family. He had not been out of his house in weeks and Aemilia had not visited him now for two weeks, put off by his constant disregard for her. You might think that she would go and tell Nicholas what was going on with her father and family, but Aemilia was very upset with Nicholas. Besides, she and her sisters were focused on doing all they could to help her parents sell their contracts and make the repayment. They were very disheartened that their hard work had only generated 1,500 denarii. They had no idea, however, what it was going to mean that they couldn't repay Alexander. They simply believed Alexander would give them an extension. Of course, that belief was ill founded.

6 – Deceived

Today was Thursday morning – the day Stephen and Faustina's payment to Alexander was due. It was about three months since Nicholas's parents died and he hadn't even realized it had been two weeks since Aemilia stopped by. In fact, Nicholas wasn't even cognizant that he was three months into his dark hole of despair. If asked, Nicholas couldn't have made a list of his visitors. His house was ill kept. Neptune was barely getting by with whatever food Nicholas didn't eat from Rufus and whatever food Neptune could find wandering around in the neighborhood. Someone had even stolen Nicholas's horse – he didn't even realize she was missing.

Nicholas heard a knock on the door. It certainly wasn't going to be the first knock that Nicholas chose to ignore.

Then the knock came a second time. This time it was louder and faster. I'm not sure that every person has a unique door knock like they have a unique fingerprint, but this knock didn't match the knocks of Aemilia or Rufus. Aemilia's knocks always came in threes, were fairly slow, and were pretty light – like she was hesitant to interrupt Nicholas. Rufus's knocks were always playful – a few rhythmic taps that sounded like a song or a rhyme. However, this knock didn't sound like either of those;

it didn't even sound like the two or three times that Papa Antony stopped by to check on Nicholas.

Finally, a voice called out, accompanying a third, even quicker and louder knock. "Nicholas! This is Alexander. We need to talk."

Being snapped back into reality for the first time in weeks, Nicholas's fog expelled from his mind as if someone turned on a light and illuminated a dark room. Nicholas suddenly felt the responsibility of a business and a business partner. In the matter of half a second, Nicholas thought that maybe this is something he needed and could do – he could turn his focus to his business – he could find something to occupy his mind.

"I'm coming Alexander."

With Nicholas opening the door, Alexander bound into the room.

"Oh, the smell! What have you let die in here?"

"I'm afraid I haven't been the best housekeeper, Alexander. Tell me, what do you want? Do you need me to start working? I'm sorry I haven't been much help, but I think I'm ready."

Nicholas spoke his words without hardly taking a breath. He didn't notice the papers in Alexander's hands or even the short, slightly round man who walked in behind Alexander.

"This is Crispus," Alexander stated. "He is a banker in Myra – a very prominent banker. Your father did business with him. We both have been doing business with Crispus for many years."

"How do you do, Nicholas?" Crispus asked, as he stretched out one hand to greet Nicholas while holding a cloth over his nose with his other hand to keep out the stench. Crispus didn't look like someone who had to deal with too many foul odors.

"Fine, thank you," Nicholas replied. Of course, he wasn't fine, but that seemed like the natural thing to say. "I remember seeing you around. You've been to some of my parents' parties."

"Crispus has some news, Nicholas, and I'm afraid it's not good news."

"I am afraid it is not good news," Crispus added, rarely using contractions and always speaking with an air of superiority. "Nicholas, your parents lost a large amount of inventory in the fire – that is in addition to the lost business transactions and broken contracts. It adds up to a significant sum of money."

"I understand," Nicholas said. "We can earn it back, right Alexander? I'm sure we can take care of it soon enough."

Alexander didn't respond. His face was a mix of sadness and disgust. Nicholas wasn't quite sure how to read him. The three stood there in an awkward silence.

Crispus broke the silence, "I am afraid you are responsible, Nicholas. Or, at least your parents were responsible. It is not Alexander's problem. It is yours." Nicholas stared blankly at Crispus as he spoke. "In fact, my calculations show that you owe 4,000 aurei."

"4,000 aurei!" Nicholas exclaimed, feeling emotion for the first time in a while. "That's 100,000 denarii. That's probably everything I have!"

Here's a little bit of a Roman money history lesson. A normal day's pay for someone like Rufus's dad would have been about two denarii a day (a single denarii is called a denarius). So, multiply that by about 300 working days and around 30 working years, and a person might expect to earn around 18,000 denarii in his lifetime. An aureus was worth 25 denarii, so 4,000 aurei was about 100,000 denarii, which was about five and a half life's wages. If this interests you in any bit, then you should read about the devaluation of Roman currency during the 3rd century (before Diocletian) and the efforts Diocletian made to stabilize prices and money during his reign.

"Nicholas, Nicholas. There, there Nicholas," Alexander recomposed his face, put on his salesman charm, and placed an arm on Nicholas's shoulder. "I just couldn't believe it when I heard it myself. I don't want to take your money, but we have to pay Crispus and the fire was your parents' responsibility. After

65

all, I just don't have that kind of money, especially with the money I've had to put into attempting to restore our inventory."

"4,000 aurei? I can't even imagine paying it. That would be everything my parents ever had." With those words, Nicholas began sobbing. It was as if all three months of emotion burst forth through the weak dam that his psyche had fragilely built.

"Oh, Nicholas," now Alexander was fully embracing him, "you are like a son to me. I feel so badly for you and all you've gone through."

"So, you have that much money, right Nicholas?" Crispus said, attempting to return the discussion to business. After all, Crispus really didn't think Nicholas would have that much money. Now, it is true that Nicholas's parents kept some accounts with Crispus and that they did actually owe him a little bit of money. However, Alexander came to Crispus a couple of weeks earlier to convince Crispus to accompany him on his visit to Nicholas. Crispus was hesitant at first, not worrying too much about the 250 denarii Nicholas's parents owed him. But, when Alexander convinced Crispus that Nicholas was truly rich and that Alexander would greatly reward him for his help, Crispus decided that Nicholas's parents might "owe" him much more than he originally figured.

"I suppose so – even though that would be all I have," Nicholas said softly.

"Well, then it is settled. You pay Alexander the money and he will take care of everything else – the accounts, the inventory, and... Oh yeah! My debts as well."

"OK," Nicholas paused. "Is it really true, Alexander? I trust you with everything I have – is it really true? 4,000 aurei?"

"I'm afraid it is true, Nicholas. In fact, there is one more thing."

Nicholas looked at Alexander as he spoke – wondering what in the world "one more thing" might mean. He glanced at Crispus – he was quickly losing trust that Crispus was an honest man – but even Crispus gave Nicholas a quick shrug, indicating he didn't know what Alexander meant.

"I'm going to ask you to leave now, Crispus," Alexander said as he grabbed Crispus by the arm and walked him to the door. "Thank you so much for your help – I'll be by tomorrow to square up our debts."

"I look forward to seeing you tomorrow, but I can stay," Crispus replied, curious what the manipulative Alexander was up to now.

"That won't be necessary. Nicholas and I need to talk shop – you know, trade secrets and such."

With that Crispus said his goodbyes and shuffled his short body out the door.

"What is it Alexander?'"

"Nicholas, we need to talk about the business. It's not doing well – it hasn't been doing well for a while."

"Do you mean since my parents died? It was doing great before then."

"No, I'm afraid it wasn't doing well even before your parents' untimely death. We've been struggling. I'm not even sure your 4,000 aurei is going to take care of it."

Nicholas didn't know what to think. Was the business really in that bad of shape? His parents were always careful with money. Their only extravagances were the large parties that Alexander convinced them to host. He wracked his brain – his dad didn't seem stressed. Was his mom acting differently? She did make a comment about Nicholas's boat and how that most boys didn't have their own boats. Was she worried about money when she said that?

"Nicholas, I cared about your parents and I care about you. To be honest, I'm really concerned about what this business might do to you. Imagine if we can't pay our debts! An old man like me – I could go to prison! But, at least I have lived a nice, full life. But you – I can't imagine…"

"Prison! What are you talking about Alexander? Is it really that bad?"

"I don't know for sure, Nicholas. Things are pretty bleak."

"I just can't believe it! I can't go to prison! What can we do?"

"I've been thinking Nicholas – thinking a lot. It's been three months since your parents passed and I've been thinking really hard. I just don't want anything to happen to you Nicholas."

With that said, Alexander paused and looked intently at Nicholas. Alexander's outward appearance was one of concern and sorrow, but on the inside Alexander's heart was racing as he was about to finish off this conversation he had been rehearsing in his mind for weeks. Of course, the business wasn't doing poorly. Sure the fire set them back, but nothing about 200 aurei couldn't fix. And, of course, things were definitely going well three months ago when Nicholas's parents were alive. And, of course, Alexander really didn't care deeply for Nicholas, despite his award-winning acting.

"Nicholas, I think the best option is for you to sign over your half of the business to me. I will do it free of charge – I won't even make you pay me for it. I just don't want to risk you going to prison. It's going to be a tough road and you shouldn't have to go through it. You're young – you have your whole life ahead of you."

Alexander practically delivered every good line he had thought of in one big breath. Nicholas was confused and bewildered. He trusted Alexander and had no doubt but to believe him. It's easy to look at Nicholas as naive, but he grew up around Alexander – Alexander was like an uncle to him. Nicholas had no reason to doubt him. Nicholas had every reason to trust his judgment.

"I don't know what to say. I don't want to leave you responsible by yourself."

"It's OK, Nicholas. I think it will be better this way. With only one owner, I might be able to go to Corinth or Ephesus and strike some deals – try to get it back on its feet."

With his speech delivered, Alexander waited for what seemed like an eternity of silence as Nicholas processed the "generous" offer.

"OK, if that's what you say I need to do."

Although it was against everything that Nicholas felt he should do, he agreed to give his half of the business to Alexander. Alexander already had the paperwork written up and he pulled out the document for Nicholas to sign. For a moment, as Nicholas was signing the papers, Alexander panicked, realizing that he should have kept Crispus around to be the witness. "No matter," he thought." I'm sure I can get Crispus to 'witness' this signing for another hundred denarii."

With the stroke of a pen, Nicholas was no longer the co-owner of a once-profitable business. And, in the next few minutes, Nicholas went into the back room and pulled out his bags of coins — one after another — until he had no bags remaining. He wasn't sure it was 4,000 aurei — he was actually afraid it wasn't enough. Alexander graciously offered to take it all and have it counted. "We'll settle up down the road," Alexander said.

Alexander took his bags of money (he had the foresight to bring a cart), he took his freshly signed contract, and he left. He was on his way to Crispus's bank and then to Stephen and Faustina's house to collect the 15,000 denarii that he knew they couldn't possibly have. "What a fun, profitable day this is!" Alexander mused in his head.

In a matter of seconds, the emptiness of the house that consumed Nicholas for the last three months washed over him once more. Although he felt like he had lost everything before, he now realized a new depth of loss and loneliness than he thought possible. This was not the time for a familiar door knock, but just a few moments later, one came anyway.

Knock, knock, knock. This knock was lighter and slower than Alexander's. Nicholas knew this one belonged to Aemilia. She wasn't even sure why she came to Nicholas's house. Her family was in trouble and she knew that Alexander would be at her house to collect his money sometime today. Perhaps she just hoped that seeing Nicholas – a miraculously improved Nicholas – would put her mind at ease about everything that was going on.

"Please go away, Aemilia."

"How do you know it's me?"

"I just do. Now please go away."

"Nick, I'm worried about you. Let me see you."

"I don't want you to see me and I don't want to see you." Now the first part was definitely true, but the last part was just Nicholas's emotion speaking.

Aemilia began to softly sob. Nicholas opened the door.

"What do you want?" Nicholas stood in the doorway, not inviting her in and trying not to let her see how bad the house looked.

"Nick, I'm worried for you. You don't come out of your house. Do you eat?"

"I'm still alive, aren't I? Even I can't be lucky enough to escape from this life through starvation."

"Oh, don't say that! You have much to live for. God still loves you, you know!"

"God?! What God do you speak of? They only God I've known I'm not even sure exists anymore."

"Don't say that," Aemilia was practically whispering. She couldn't believe her ears – Nicholas was so hurt and so cold toward her.

"Well, it's true. I've been thinking about it Aemilia. God sure hasn't helped me – I kind of doubt that there is any type of god anymore."

"Just because you aren't sure doesn't make it so. God is there, whether you want to believe it or not."

Aemilia waited for a response, but Nicholas just shuffled his feet a bit and then went over and sat down. Aemilia walked toward him, moved a pile of clothes, and sat down beside him. She wanted to talk about her trouble, but didn't think he had the capacity for compassion.

"Nick, think back to the good times – you believed in God then. Do you think that God only exists in the good times?"

Still no response. Nicholas's eyes started to tear up. Aemilia couldn't tell if Nicholas was coming around or getting angry.

"I mean, God has blessed you in so…"

"God hasn't blessed me!" Nicholas was furious and unleashed on Aemilia in a fit of rage she had never seen him have before.

"God has taken away everything that I love – my parents, my father's business, my money! I don't care if there is a god and you can call him Jesus or Zeus or my dog, Neptune, if you want! I don't want anything to do with that god and if you're going to sit here and lecture me about it, then I don't want anything to do with you either!"

Aemilia was shocked. Now the tears that were already forming in her eyes started slowly rolling down her face. She paused uncomfortably, frozen, hoping that Nicholas would soften and apologize. Instead, he seemed resolute in his anger and his disdain for her.

"This isn't who you are Nicholas." That was the first time she called him by his full first name since they were children. "The man who I see before me today is not the man who I know."

"This is who I am, Aemilia. I'm sorry to disappoint you. I think you should leave."

"I don't know if I'll be back, Nicholas."

Nicholas didn't respond. He stared off to the side, ignoring her threat to leave him for good. With Nicholas acting like he didn't notice, Aemilia rose from the couch, walked to the door, slowly opened it, and walked out.

*** *** *** *** *** *** *** *** *** *** ***

Aemilia walked the short distance home with blurry

tears, hardly able to see her feet walking one in front of the other. She sobbed uncontrollably and must have looked hysterical to anyone she passed.

Aemilia's mind raced with thoughts – often conflicting thoughts.

"What is he thinking?"
"I think he's changed forever."
"That's not the real Nicholas."
"I could never marry him."
"He is hurting so badly."
"I need to find a way to help him."
"I've never had someone hurt me so badly."
"What have I done? What is wrong with me? It must be my fault."

She lost both her best friend and the man she thought she might marry. "I'm going to be like Diantha," she thought, "old and without any possible man who wants to marry me." That wasn't quite fair to Diantha, but Diantha certainly didn't do herself any favors with how she acted superior to any man who might have been remotely interested in her.

Aemilia arrived home, her walk taking what seemed to be both minutes and hours at the same time. Right before she walked through the front door, she tried to compose herself. She badly wanted to talk to her mother about what happened, but she really didn't want her sisters to see her so upset and she knew that they all had other things to worry about today.

Walking through the front door, she saw her mom seated across the room. She started across the room toward her, but then saw both of her sisters standing off to her right. In an instant she decided she'd walk past her mother and go into her bedroom, until she saw her father sitting off to the left. Everyone was silent and quietly crying. She paused, looked at each of them one by one, and stood in the center of the room.

"What is going on? Did Alexander come?" she asked.

Unfortunately for Aemilia, her day was about to get much worse.

Aemilia looked at each member of her family in their living room. No one was talking and they were each crying in their own way. Her mother was letting out little sobs, rhythmically in pairs of twos. Diantha was trying to be strong, but her stoic look was compromised by the tear stains on her cheeks. Iris was sniffling and crying – she was definitely the most out of control. And even her father had tears in his eyes, though no stained cheeks, sobs, or sniffles.

Aemilia had been crying too – crying because of her family's situation and crying because of Nicholas's rejection (she couldn't even tell him what was going on with her family – he was too cold and focused on himself).

Aemilia knew her father was going to ask Alexander for an extension and she had every reason to believe that he would give it. After all, he had been so kind to loan them the money in the first place. Ever the optimist, Aemilia figured that maybe Alexander's hard heart was softening since the death of his business partner.

Aemilia again broke the tearful silence. "What is going on?" she asked.

Iris began to cry loudly and uncontrollably. Her mother wouldn't look up and her father seemed like he couldn't speak. Diantha spoke up, "That evil man won't give us an extension. He's requiring the money today!"

"But we don't have the money," Iris was speaking loudly while crying, "and now he has threatened to have us all sold!"

"Sold?! What are you talking about, Iris? Have you gone crazy?" Aemilia knew her sister usually overreacted. Certainly that explained her irrationality now.

"It's true, Aemilia. He's going to have us all sold! I'll probably be sold to some old, fat guy who stinks and likes to eat nothing but turnips," Iris sobbed.

"Mom, Dad, what's going on?" Aemilia asked.

Her mom cried even louder. Her dad took a deep breath, and began to talk.

"My agreement with Alexander was that I would repay him in one week. It's what I had to do. I haven't been able to pay it and now Alexander is demanding the money."

"That evil man. Who does he think he is? He is so sneaky and mean. I wish he were dead!" Diantha exclaimed.

"Diantha, don't talk like that," Stephen replied.

Aemilia brought the conversation back to her confusion. "What's this that Iris is blabbing about – selling us?"

Stephen continued explaining, "Under Roman law, if a parent can't pay their debt, then the debtor can sell the parent's children as payment for the debt. Alexander…" Stephen finally started crying, not able to finish his thought.

"What? I can't believe it? This can't be happening! Certainly, there's something we can do. Can't we sell our house, our animals, the business, anything?" Aemilia was finally catching up to the shock and grief her family had been experiencing for the last five minutes. She must have just missed passing Alexander on the street. It turns out that he was at her house while she was at Nicholas's house; which, of course, he had just been at Nicholas's house prior to that, taking Nicholas's money and half of the business.

"Honcy, we will do everything we can. We will find a way. God will provide a way. There's no way I'm losing you."

For the rest of the evening, the family sat together and cried together. They weren't a perfect family, but they loved each other. Stephen would gladly stay in prison, lose his house, or even face execution to protect his daughters. Faustina was beside herself. She wondered if Stephen tried hard enough to sell his contracts or if she should have done more to help manage the business in the first place. Diantha spent the evening offering idea after idea – ways to get the money or flee town. Iris spent most of the evening imagining every possible worst scenario of where she would end up as a sold young woman. By the end of the night, she had herself sold to a trio of made-up giants who never took baths and ate uncooked rabbits for dinner.

Roman law required that children, sold as slaves, could replace large sums of unpaid debts. Of course, Alexander knew this law going into his scheme. In fact, he knew that Roman law allowed for 5,000 denarii per sold child, so it is no coincidence that Stephen's fine was 15,000 denarii. Alexander made sure that the magistrate saw to that.

Slavery in the late third century was reemerging in popularity. For the most part, it declined in use and number of slaves from the early first century to the early third century. However, about 70 years before our story, the Roman economy began having problems with inflation and debt, and so slavery reversed its decline. Unfortunately, many people resorted to giving themselves and their families to slavery as a way to pay off their debts.

The law didn't allow a person's children to be taken at the same time and it required the contract breaker be given five days to repay the money before his children were taken. So, according to law, Alexander would have to wait five days, then he could seize Diantha. Then on the sixth day he could seize Iris and on the seventh day he could seize Aemilia. He thought about keeping Aemilia for himself – he thought that would be the cherry on top of his evil scheme. "Imagine Nicholas – losing his everything and his girl!" he thought. "And besides, the idea of Stephen knowing his daughter was still in town and seeing her clean a house or take out the trash would rub it in a little bit harder."

Of course, if Stephen could come up with the money in the next five days, then his daughters would be safe. He didn't even have to have all of the money by day five on Tuesday. As long as he had the first 5,000 denarii by Tuesday for Diantha, the next 5,000 denarii by Wednesday for Iris, and the last 5,000 denarii by Thursday for Aemilia, then all would be well. It would be up to Alexander to make sure Stephen couldn't get that money in the next seven days. He had already kept him from getting the money so far and he was confident he could keep it up. The best news was that law prohibited Stephen from borrowing money to pay back borrowed money. No one could help Stephen, even though you remember Alexander had helped him before. Don't forget, Alexander paid off the magistrate when he helped Stephen in the first place and paid a little extra to make sure that no one else could do the same.

While Stephen, Faustina, and the girls cried and talked and tried to figure out a plan, that night Alexander hardly slept. He didn't feel guilty or bad, he just couldn't believe that his plan was working so well. His mind raced with thoughts of how Nicholas must feel – poor and without a business. He thought about the work he needed to keep doing over the next week to keep Stephen from getting the 15,000 denarii. And, he thought about how sad Stephen and his family must be. "Revenge is sweet. And winning is sweeter," he thought to himself as he finally drifted asleep.

7 – The Spiral

    Nicholas had been having many dark days and nights, but this particular evening was probably his worst. In the matter of a couple of hours he lost his fortune, his father's business, and the woman he thought he might love. Such depths of despair plays cruel tricks on the mind. Nicholas kept spiraling deeper and deeper into the depths of his emptiness and sorrow. He was unsure how to go about his life. He wasn't even sure he wanted to go about his life.
    This is not who Nicholas was, it was just who he was at this moment. Our moments don't define us as people – the sum of our moments define us. It's never a good idea to judge a person based on how you find them on any one day. That would be like opening a book to the middle, reading one page, and making a judgment about what the book is about and if it is any good.
    We wouldn't be learning about the story of Nicholas if this one moment defined him. On this page, he is not only a miserable person, but pretty unlovable too.
    That's not who Nicholas was before his parents died. Nicholas might have been a little naive, but he was anything but negative. Nicholas had a great outlook on life. Most of his peers

thought of him as the "perfect kid" – they might have made fun of him, but most of them wished they were more like him. He always had friends (and many of them were genuine); he had parents who loved him; he was rich; he was smart; and he was kind. He not only got along well with kids, but also with adults. As he was becoming an adult himself, he found himself confident at his parents' parties – able to make small talk about politics or serious talk about religion.

Nicholas was a little bit naive, however. It wasn't his fault. It was just the ramifications of having so much in life come easily for him. Take Rufus, for example. Rufus knew a little more about how the real world worked – some people were dishonest and most people really had their own interests in mind. It wasn't because Rufus was a bad person or a pessimist; it's just that his life – full of hard work and scraping by – gave him life experiences that Nicholas hadn't had to encounter yet.

Even Aemilia had a better understanding of trouble and pain – she at least had sisters. While her life was mostly easy like Nicholas's life, she did have two older sisters to contend with. And, it doesn't matter how great a set of siblings' relationships are, they still experience arguments and frustrations that an only child like Nicholas never has to suffer through. Even something as simple as which child gets to talk to her mother when they all are upset is one small example of something someone with siblings has to experience that an only child doesn't have to experience.

So, when a 19-year old's worst life experiences were a broken sail on his boat or a dog that was sick through the night, something like dead parents not only rocks his world, but it shakes the very core and foundation of what he thought his world was made of.

It's no wonder that Nicholas's faith in God was also so deeply rocked in these last three months. His parents' faith was one born out of humble beginnings and years of barrenness. Their faith allowed them to find a trust in God that was genuine and forged through the hot flames of hardship and trouble.

Nicholas's faith in God was a faith of easiness. He believed in God because that is what his parents did and he didn't have any reason not to accept it too. Up until now, he hadn't had the hard moments in life that his parents experienced that shaped their faith and deepened their faith in God. Those hard experiences are the kinds of moments that we set up as memorial stones deep in our brains – memorial stones that remind us we can trust in God and that he has been faithful in the past.

Now the very truths that Nicholas based his entire life on were washed away as if in a flash flood. A flash flood comes from seemingly nowhere, as the often-ignored creeks and rivers that run beside our everyday lives suddenly fill way beyond their banks, quickly ascending feet above where we could have possibly imagined they could reach. In an instant they climb to unimaginable heights; in an instant they do a great amount of destruction; and in an instant they retreat back to their banks – leaving behind death and debris, and leaving their seemingly indelible marks.

But, the marks of flash floods are only seemingly indelible because eventually the debris fades and the destruction is repaired or replaced. The floods are all but forgotten and their effects drift farther away and fade farther into memory.

Like a flash flood, Nicholas's world had been destroyed swiftly and seemingly out of nowhere. The foundation of his world, that he thought was firm and solidly built on rock, washed away like a sand castle at high tide, with no recognizable trace of what it used to be.

Nicholas could not place his despair into words. He experienced a combination of loneliness and emptiness, although the truth is that he actually felt very little of anything at all.

Aemilia was gone for good; he was sure of that. He knew he was quite rude to her, but he felt very little in the way of remorse.

Knock, kn-kn-knock, knock.
It had to be Rufus.

"Of course it is Rufus," Nicholas thought. Nicholas was convinced that Rufus could be married with a dozen children and he'd still come knocking at Nicholas's door. For most friendships, that is a welcome sign of true loyalty and love. For the current state that Nicholas was in, it was annoying and even maddening.

Rufus followed Nicholas practically everywhere and was interested in just about anything Nicholas was interested in. In some way, hanging out with Nicholas was Rufus's escape – his way to forget his family's poverty and his father's harshness.

It's true that Rufus's dad was a hard worker, but his hardness also permeated just about every other part of his life. Himself, the son of a father who worked hard to barely get by, Rufus's dad had been working since he was 14 years old and had lived by himself since he was 16 years old.

To say that Rufus's dad didn't love Rufus would be incorrect. And, it would also be wrong to paint him as abusive or neglectful. He was just harsh – harsh in his words, harsh in his mood, and harsh in his punishments.

When Rufus was just six years old he put on his dad's shoes late one evening to go play outside. As a young boy he looked up to his dad and wanted to pretend that he was his father, hard at work on the docks. Rufus didn't behave any differently than a normal six year old would behave, but as bad luck would have it, Rufus tore a hole in his dad's shoes while he was out playing.

Rufus was moving sticks from one side of the road to the other, pretending he was unloading a grand ship that had just arrived from Rome. He wasn't watching where he was going and ran his foot along the side of a splintered board. The sharp edge tore a two-inch gash through the shoe and ripped open Rufus's skin.

Crying, Rufus stumbled up the steps and into his home. Ignoring Rufus's tears, his father was first furious when he saw Rufus wearing his shoes and then even more furious when he saw the tear in the shoe's side. And, unfortunately for Rufus, the blood on his foot didn't appease his dad's anger, but made him even more mad when he realized his only pair of shoes were not just torn, but blood stained as well.

"I'm sorry, Daddy," the young boy said, quickly learning to forget his own pain to appease his father's wrath.

"Rufus! You've gone and ruined my shoes! How am I supposed to go to work with torn shoes? I should feed you to the pigs!"

"I can fix them tonight," Rufus's mom interjected. "Even if I have to stay up all night."

"This wouldn't happen if you kept an eye on him like you're supposed to!" his father shot back. "If you could do anything right, then I wouldn't have ripped shoes."

Like every other time before, that sent Rufus's mom crying off to the side of the room and sent Rufus off crying as well. He ran outside, barefoot and bleeding, trying to learn to never wear his dad's shoes again and to never put his mom in the place where his dad yelled at her because of something he did.

Through the years, hanging out with Nicholas's family was a breath of fresh air for Rufus. He didn't realize that fathers could be loving and kind, like Epiphanius was to Nicholas. Epiphanius even showed that same kindness to Rufus. Rufus loved hanging out with Nicholas's family. Nicholas never quite realized why Rufus loved his family so much. Nicholas never had a reason to think about it because he never knew a family's love to be much of any other way. Most of the time Nicholas was just happy to have such a loyal friend.

Knock, kn-kn-knock, knock. Kn-kn-knock.

"Go away, Rufus," Nicholas spoke from his couch, not opening the door.

Rufus didn't care much for doors or the manners that people usually use with them. He opened the door and walked in.

"I'm not going anywhere, Nick."

"I can't do it today Rufus. I'm not going fishing. I'm not going to the barn. I'm not going sailing. And I don't want anything to eat."

"Good thing, Nick. I wasn't planning on any of those things."

"I don't need anything, Rufus."

The truth was, Nicholas hadn't eaten in three or four days. He barely drank enough water to stay hydrated. And, given the day's events, it didn't seem likely that he would be eating much any time soon.

"Nick, I don't know what to do. I feel bad for you, buddy. What you need is to just get up and get out. Let's get some fresh air."

"Not happening, Rufus. I'm just going to sit here."

"Nick, while you're busy sitting here, the world around you is still going on. You've got a business to r…"

"I don't have a business, Rufus! It's all gone!" Nicholas raised his voice.

"Don't be silly, Nick. I think being cooped up in this house is getting to you."

"I'm not being silly. It's all gone. My money, my business, Aemilia."

"Now you might be right about that. If you keep on treating Aemilia like this, there's no telling how much longer she's going to keep coming around." Rufus didn't know that Nicholas had just lost his money and business. And, like Nicholas, he also didn't know anything that Aemilia and her family were going through.

"It doesn't matter. It's all gone. It's better if she doesn't come around."

"What's gone, Nick? I know you lost your parents – I can't even imagine what that's like – but you still have so much."

"No, I don't." Nicholas explained to Rufus everything that happened to him that day. He started with Alexander and the banker, and he explained how he had to pay just about every denarii he had. Then he explained how Alexander was looking out for him and let Nicholas sign away his half of the business, just to protect him. When he told him that, Rufus mumbled something under his breath, but Nicholas didn't hear it. Last he explained how Aemilia came over and how he treated her. He said it as a matter of fact, not with remorse or even much care that he might not see her again.

Nicholas actually started to feel a little better, explaining his day's events to Rufus. It was the most he had talked to anyone about anything for the last few months. But, just when he actually started to feel a little relief, he quickly snapped back into the mire of his situation. Almost instantly the life that was beginning to flourish in his conversation withered away and he sunk deeper into his chair and looked away from Rufus.

"Buddy, I just want to help you. I'm sorry all of that happened and I can't imagine what it's like. But, I'm here for you. You can get a job with me and my dad, and…"

"Just leave me alone, Rufus."

"Come on, Nick. It's all going to work out."

This time Nicholas spoke softer, almost whispering, "Just leave me alone, Rufus."

"Nick, I can't do it. I won't leave you alone."

Nicholas hadn't felt many emotions the last several weeks, but like earlier with Aemilia, an intense rage swelled up inside him. It burned in him like a volcano waiting thousands of years to finally erupt. "Get out, Rufus!" Nicholas yelled. "I don't want your help. I don't want your job. LEAVE ME ALONE!"

"Fine, have it your way!" Rufus angrily shot back. He was a loyal friend and would put up with about anything from Nicholas, but he wasn't having any more of it tonight. He stormed out the door and didn't even shut it. It had just started to rain and it splashed inside the house. Nicholas paid no attention – staring at the wall, seething in an anger that he could not explain and he could not expel.

Moments after Rufus left, Nicholas got up from the couch and ran out the door.

It was raining pretty steadily. Being December, the weather was often rainy. When it wasn't raining, there were usually more cloudy days than sunny days. The weather in Myra never got too cold, but December was one of the worst months – chilly at night and lots of rain.

Nicholas ran fast. He wasn't chasing after Rufus, he was just running. Maybe he was running from his feelings; maybe he was running from his life. He wanted to escape and it was as if he thought that if he ran fast enough or far enough then he might be able to outrun his troubles.

Nicholas ran out of his neighborhood. While his neighborhood had seemed safe and comfortable for so much of his life, it now felt empty and worthless. As he left his neighborhood, he started running toward the center of town. His run slowed to a jog. He passed temples and the government buildings. It was almost dark now; the streets were fairly empty because it was late and raining.

Once in the town center, Nicholas stopped. He looked backward in the direction of his house. He didn't want to go there; he didn't feel like he belonged there. He looked toward the direction of the barn. There was no reason to go to the barn – for that matter there wasn't a barn and if there was, it wouldn't even be his. He looked toward the ocean – maybe he could just get in his boat and go away. But, he knew that was a dumb idea. Even though he didn't really want to be alive, he also didn't really want to die. A single person in a small boat on the sea in December would be a sure way to tempt death's fate.

So, he turned the only other direction he could, toward the mountains. He couldn't see them because of the rain, but he knew they were there.

"The cabin," he said – out loud so that if anyone was actually nearby, then they could hear him.

Nicholas thought of his father's cabin. He thought of escape. He thought of solitude. He thought of living his life there – away from people and money and business. He thought he could escape from Alexander – how disappointed Alexander must be in him. He thought he could escape from Aemilia – how disappointed Aemilia must be in him. And he thought he could escape from Rufus – how disappointed Rufus must be in him.

It started to rain harder and the new intensity of the rain jolted Nicholas out of his frozen state in the center of town. He started walking toward the mountains. "I'll escape," he thought. "I'll escape to the cabin."

As he walked down the road he passed the beggar – the same one he passed when he ran to church the day his parents died and the same one he saw when he and Aemilia went to the barn the day after the funeral. For some reason, Nicholas reached into his pocket and found a coin. He didn't know why it was there or even how much it was. The beggar was hunched against the side of a building, barely avoiding the downpour.

"Here you go," Nicholas said as he tossed the coin. He didn't even toss the coin hard enough to make it to the beggar – it landed a couple of feet short. Yelling to the beggar through the rain, Nicholas proclaimed, "We are brothers! Brothers in misery and brothers in the darkness of this godless world!"

Nicholas laughed as he passed the beggar.

The next set of buildings belonged to the temple of Artemis Eleuthera. She was the Greek goddess of the forest and the hunt. Despite Diocletian's edicts for people to be more Roman, Greek gods were allowed because they were closely related to Roman gods. When Nicholas and his father would ever walk down this street (usually on the way to the cabin), his father would make Nicholas walk quickly and shield his eyes. There were often temple workers, slaves really, who would be scantily dressed, trying to lure people inside. There were no such workers this late evening in the rain. Nicholas looked at the temple indifferently – thinking all religion is a waste of time.

A few minutes later he passed an orphanage – not really an orphanage like we might think, but a building where a couple of area churches tried to provide for orphans. Papa Antony and his wife were among the primary people who worked to ensure the children had food and a place to stay. Nicholas hardly even knew the place existed in Myra – he had heard about it and had obviously seen it before, but it was never really on his radar. As he walked by the building, even in the heavy rain he could hear children laughing. "What have they got to laugh about?" he thought. "Even the orphans have more in this world than I do."

The orphans' laughter deflated Nicholas's energetic determination to get up the mountain. For the first time, he realized he was cold, walking in the rain, and hungry. He slumped his shoulders, and walked out of Myra.

There was nothing about Nicholas's plan that was logical. It was about six in the evening and raining – and Nicholas had set out for his father's cabin. He had never walked there before – every other time that he went he and his dad took a horse or even a horse and a wagon.

It was only a 13-mile walk – that is how close the mountains are to Myra and the sea. But, with the elevation change one could expect that 13-mile walk to take at least 10 hours. Considering the rain and the dark, Nicholas was quite foolish for setting out on this journey on foot in the evening.

After just an hour, there was barely any light left to see. Nicholas was well out of Myra now and making good time. The first couple of miles were fairly flat and dotted by farms and houses. Any hope Nicholas might have had of moonlight or starlight was covered by the clouds that provided the nagging downfall of rain. Nevertheless, Nicholas pressed on.

After another hour, Nicholas joined up with the river that flowed down the mountains and into the sea. The path up the mountains and to his cabin followed the river. It was a well-worn path that existed for hundreds of years before Nicholas was born and has persisted these several hundreds of years since his death.

About four hours later, Nicholas decided to take a break. He was truly exhausted – it was around midnight. The rain took a temporary reprieve and the moon was trying to peak between the thick clouds. Nicholas's eyes had adjusted well to the dark and the light of the moon gave him more than enough light to see a rock ledge that he decided to stop and sit on.

Sitting down, Nicholas truly felt his weariness. It was as if continuing to move had kept his muscles going fast enough that his brain couldn't catch up and figure out how tired he was. Now that he sat down, he felt his aches and suffered from the effects of not eating these last few days.

The clouds might have been clearing, but Nicholas's head was not. He kept running through a flurry of thoughts – none of them helpful or constructive.

"Why would God do this to me?"

"What is my life even about?"

"I'll just stay alone the rest of my life – a hermit in these mountains."

"I bet no one cares – no one will even know I'm gone."

"It truly is best for Aemilia that I'm gone. She needs someone better than me."

"Rufus, stupid Rufus. He needs to give up on me and do something with his life."

With these thoughts swirling in his head, Nicholas fell asleep on the rock.

*** *** *** *** *** *** *** *** *** ***

Sometime later – it had to be a couple of hours, Nicholas woke up as the rain restarted and began pounding against his face. Half confused as to where he was, Nicholas stumbled up from the rock and started walking again.

This time, Nicholas's walk was less steady, but he was persistent. He walked one hour after waking up, slowly trekking up the mountain, along the well-worn path, following the creek. Then, a second hour passed and Nicholas was still walking up the mountain. Sometime, during the third hour, the rain transitioned into snow. The flakes were large and very wet, almost like large, slightly frozen rain drops. They looked like snow, but when they hit Nicholas's clothes or hair, they immediately melted and applied a fresh layer of cold water to his already soaked body.

Soon, the snow became well defined and a thick layer of it covered Nicholas's path. It was very late in the night and there certainly weren't other footprints or wagon prints to mark the trail for him. In a matter of minutes, Nicholas found himself drudging through an inch of snow, barely able to make out the path.

After an hour of snow and not long before daylight, Nicholas was walking through two to three inches of snow. While he wasn't always sure he was on the path, the nearby river kept him on course. Nicholas was more than tired; he was more than exhausted. He couldn't keep thoughts in his head. He was cold. He was hungry. He was emotionally drained. He was physically drained.

It wasn't long before Nicholas's barely-coherent thoughts turned to death. "What if this is it? Maybe this is how it's supposed to end."

Nicholas tripped and fell to the ground – he couldn't see the tree branch lying across the path with the snow covering it.

Nicholas barely had the strength to get back up, but somehow he managed. He stood up, stepped over the branch, and kept walking.

Just three steps, maybe four, and then he fell again.

His lips were chapped – partially dehydrated and partially too cold. Nicholas didn't prepare for December in the mountains – he was barely dressed appropriately for December in Myra.

Nicholas pulled himself to his knees. He grabbed a scoopful of snow and ate it, thirsty and hungry. "The cabin can't be much farther, can it?" Nicholas thought. Everything looked the same in the snow – and it was still dark.

Nicholas stood up and took a few more steps. It seemed as if the snow was falling down and up and left and right. The world began to spin. The river near the path sounded louder than before. He slipped again. This time he didn't get back up.

His eyes closed and he drifted into somewhere between sleep and unconsciousness.

8 – Redeemed

The mountains that push Myra up against the sea are large and foreboding. They cut off Myra from the rest of Lycia, with the exception of two major roads that cut through the mountains along the valleys carved by rivers and a small number of other paths and trails that also largely follow rivers and creeks. That is one reason why boating on the Mediterranean Sea was so prevalent in Myra – it was a critical means of transportation – the only effective way to move people and resources to other towns and provinces.

While Myra itself was situated on a flat stretch of fertile ground, it was literally squeezed between the sea and the mountains. That is why some of Myra's most unique structures aren't stand-alone buildings, but rather buildings that were cut straight into adjacent mountainsides. Those mountains are steep and rise quickly in elevation, creating a God-made barrier of protection around the city.

In fact, one of the most enduring architectural features that has survived to this day are two sets of tombs cut into the mountains on the edge of the city. Ornately decorated and previously colorful, it is estimated that Myran people built the tombs about a hundred years after our story. In fact, as prominent as Nicholas's family was in Myra, there's a good chance that they would have been buried in the tombs if this story took place a hundred or so years later.

The path Nicholas took into the mountains wasn't too strenuous. Yes, it consistently climbed in elevation, but it was a well-worn path that was generally free of debris. During the first few miles, there were actually nicely-built bridges over the side creeks that fed into the river. Further up into the mountains the bridges were replaced by less secure structures, usually planed trees lying side by side, often tied together with sailing rope.

Nicholas's cabin was just off the main path that wound along the river. It wasn't visible from the main path – you had to know where to turn off the path, hike about 100 yards, and then you were there. It was a secluded cabin, hidden both by the dense woods and the sound of the nearby river. Nicholas's father owned most of that particular ridge; he had traded for it years ago in a textile deal.

Nicholas loved coming up to the cabin with his father. One of his earliest memories of going into the mountains with his father was one November when they visited the cabin, only to be unexpectedly stuck there by a late fall snowfall. Nicholas was a young boy – probably six or seven, and they had taken a horse with a small cart to the cabin. Nicholas's dad used the cart to take supplies to the cabin for the winter and also used the cart to take some logs back home. The sudden snow was too deep for the cart, and Epiphanius felt it was too dangerous to try to go all the way back home in the snow with a young boy.

Those two nights stuck in the cabin were a special time to Nicholas. His dad tried to cook whatever food he could find – they truly might have starved if they had to depend on Epiphanius's cooking for much longer than a few days. Nicholas didn't mind though, because his father told him stories about his own childhood, stories about sailors, stories about Greek and Roman gods, stories from the Bible, and stories about ancient Greek battles.

The story that Nicholas always remembered was a story about his great grandfather, the man who first owned the gold necklace.

"Let me tell you a story about *my* grandpappy," Epiphanius motioned toward the young boy to come and sit on his lap. They had just finished two very unrewarding bowls of turnip soup, though Nicholas thought there was nothing better in the world than being stuck in that cabin with his father.

"Your great grandpappy's name was Gregorius, which means to be watchful or alert. It's neat, Nicholas, how that parents name a child when he is first born, not knowing anything about what that child will grow up to be. But yet, people often tend to become their name."

"What does 'watchful' mean, Daddy?"

"Well, I suppose that watchful can mean a lot of things. I like to think of someone being watchful if they look out for other people. Maybe they take care of people."

"Was great grandpappy watchful, Daddy?" Nicholas looked up at his father, soaking in every last word.

"Yes, that is a good way to describe him. You see, he was very watchful over your great grandma, my grandmother, Sophia. I never knew her, my grandma."

"Why not? Did she pass away before you met her?" Nicholas didn't really know much about death, but he knew that he didn't know his grandparents because they both had 'passed away.' In fact, the young Nicholas didn't really understand what they passed or where away was, but he thought it had something to do with heaven.

"Well, it is true that she is passed away now, but that is not why I never knew her. You see your great grandpappy and great grandma married secretly. They weren't allowed to get married – they both believed in God and went to church, but that was during a time when some people didn't like it if you went to church. Your great grandma's family would never allow her to marry your great grandpappy, but they loved each other so much that they got married anyway."

"Wow..."

"They kept their marriage a secret, until God decided to let your great grandma get pregnant."

"She had Grandpappy Timothy!" Nicholas was starting to put things together, figuring out in his young brain the basics of ancestry.

"Yes, Nicholas, with Grandpappy Timothy. But, not just Grandpappy Timothy – your great grandma was pregnant with twins!"

"Twins! Wow..." Nicholas had only seen one pair of twins in his entire life. They were a pair of older girls who always dressed the same and wore their hair the same.

"Yes, twins. But the story is kind of sad. You see, your great grandma's parents found out about their secret marriage when she became pregnant."

"How come? How did they find out?"

"Well, when God let's a woman become pregnant, her baby – or in this case two babies – grows inside her belly. That makes her belly get bigger and bigger. Most people can tell when a woman is pregnant. Though, here's a word of advice, son, don't ever tell a woman she looks like she must be pregnant!"

"OK, daddy," Nicholas didn't understand why his father chuckled.

"Anyway, to make a long story a little shorter, she gave birth to Timothy, your grandpappy, and a little girl. Great Grandpappy Gregorius and Great Grandma Sophia met one night, late, just before Sophia's parents were taking her far away to Macedonia because they didn't want her and your great grandpappy to be together. So, that last night that they saw each other, they decided that they would each raise one of their children. Your great grandpappy raised your grandpappy, and your great grandma raised the little girl – I've never even known her name."

"Did they ever see each other again?"

"No, Nicholas. Your great grandpappy and great grandma never saw each other again. And, your grandpappy, Timothy, never met his twin."

"Huh." Nicholas thought for a second. "What does my name mean?" Nicholas wanted to learn more about his great grandfather, but his short attention span left the fascinating story of his grandpa and turned back to the meaning of names.

"Nicholas, your name is the combination of two names – 'Niko' and 'Laos.' Those two words mean 'victory' and 'people.'"

"Does that mean I'm going to be a great warrior?" Nicholas hopped off his dad's lap and swung around his pretend sword.

"I don't know Nicholas, but anyone should consider it an honor for their life if they can bring victory to people in any way or fashion. That's my prayer for you Nicholas, that you will bring victory to people."

As he grew older, Nicholas often thought about that conversation with his father. He thought about it when he was proud of something he did and he thought about it when he was disappointed in himself. And, of course, Nicholas remembered it every time he went to the cabin.

While growing up, Nicholas often traveled to the cabin with his father, though sometimes his father went alone. The cabin was Epiphanius's escape – his opportunity to refresh and refocus, his opportunity to take time to think and plan and dream. Nicholas had even come to the cabin a small number of times with only Rufus, having a guys' time where they hunted and fished, and talked about life and girls. Nicholas's favorite retreat was his boat, but as he got older and grew into manhood, his fondness for his father's cabin grew and he better appreciated his dad's love for it.

*** *** *** *** *** *** *** *** *** *** ***

Nicholas was lying down and barely opened his eyes – he was weak and the dim light revealed to him how badly his head was hurting. He wasn't sure where he was. He really wasn't conscious enough to even wonder where he was.

A voice spoke softly, "Take it easy. Try to rest."

It was a familiar voice, but Nicholas was too exhausted to think about it. He closed his eyes and tried to say something, but fell back asleep.

*** *** *** *** *** *** *** *** *** *** ***

Nicholas awoke a few hours later, still barely cognizant of his surroundings. He partly opened his eyes – he was indoors, lying on something soft. There was a small light in the room – it seemed to be from a fire. He tried to speak, but couldn't summon the energy.

He had a memory, or a piece of a memory. Someone (who?) helping him up – out of the snow.

"That's right," he remembered, "I was hiking in the snow." He was going to his father's cabin – that part was just coming back to him.

He remembered something else – someone (who?) talking and practically carrying him. It was so cold. He was so hungry and tired and thirsty.

Nicholas fell back asleep. Although his conscious was extremely dim and unreliable, his subconscious provided a vivid, realistic dream while he slept.

*** *** *** *** *** *** *** *** *** *** ***

Nicholas was at the barn – the barn was unburnt, but Nicholas knew he was there the day after his parents' funeral. It was cloudy and windy – no sun and no rain. There were no people anywhere; he was alone – Aemilia and Rufus weren't with him this time.

Nicholas walked through the front doors and proceeded to the three holes. The first two holes were uncovered. He peered into the first one and saw Alexander counting his father's money – laughing and counting loudly. He walked to the second hole, looked in, and saw Crispus, the banker, licking his hands as if he had just eaten a fattening meal and didn't want any part of it to go to waste.

Nicholas headed to the third hole. When he got to it, he looked down at the covered, third hole and then he looked back up. Immediately the barn that he was standing in was completely burnt and the third hole looked just as it did the day Nicholas discovered it. It was covered in debris and Nicholas immediately stooped down and began to uncover the whole.

"Need any help, Nick," Rufus asked.

"Nope, I'm good."

Nicholas immediately stood straight up and looked around – there was no Rufus.

He knelt back down and uncovered the wooden cover, reached down and pried it off the ground. Nicholas tossed it to the side. "Sorry, Aemilia," Nicholas said, sensing he had just barely missed hitting her with the wooden cover. Again, Nicholas stood up and looked around – there was no Aemilia.

Nicholas looked into the hole, deciding if he should go in. He felt a hand on his shoulder. Nicholas looked to his side and saw an older man with white hair and white facial hair. Nicholas had never seen his great-grandfather before, but he knew that's who it was.

"Go into the hole, Nicholas. See what is there."

Nicholas looked at the man. His face was so warm and full of compassion and love. Nicholas felt safe in his presence. He looked at the hole and then back toward the man – he was gone.

Nicholas let himself down into the hole. It looked like what he remembered – no money and no gold necklace. Actually, the only things he saw were a couple of coins on the floor. Nicholas stood in place, but looked all around the room.

It looked plain and empty. It even felt plain and empty. It felt like the way his house felt for the last three months.

"Nicholas, help us."

Nicholas heard a faint whisper.

"Nicholas, help us."

This time it was a little bit louder, a little bit bolder, and with a little bit more urgency. It was the voice of a woman – a familiar woman.

This time a man's voice spoke, even louder. "Nicholas, son, help us!"

It was Nicholas's parents and the sound was coming from the wooden floor of the tiny room! Nicholas reached down and slipped his fingers between planks of the wood and began ripping up the floor.

"Mom? Dad? I'm coming! I'll be right there!"

Nicholas ripped up board after board, tossing them to the side, crashing each board into one of the wooden beams that supported the room.

Finally, after ripping up six boards, Nicholas lowered his body down through the hole.

"I'm coming! It's Nicholas! I'm coming! I'll be right there!"

Nicholas landed on the floor of this new, second room, below the first room.

"Mom, Dad? Where are you?"

Silence. No one was there.

"Dad? Please, it's Nicholas! I'm here. Where are you?"

No response.

Nicholas sat down on the floor, placed his head in his hands, and cried.

After a few seconds of crying, Nicholas raised his head and looked around the second room, still sitting on the floor. This room was full of torches attached to the walls – two torches per wall, except for the fourth wall. It had four torches – two attached to the wall like the other three walls, but then two more tilted to form an X, situated above a chest.

Nicholas wiped away his tears, forgetting he heard his parents' voices. He got up and walked toward the chest – the torches were inviting him to open the chest.

He reached down – it was locked. Nicholas jiggled the lock and tried to pry open the chest, but he couldn't.

For a reason Nicholas couldn't explain, he reached into his pocket and felt something – a key. He pulled out the key, placed it into the chest, and opened it up. Inside was his father's dirty, brownish, red coat – the same one Nicholas found at the barn with Aemilia and Rufus.

In disgust, Nicholas threw it back into the chest and slammed the lid.

"It is cold – put it on." Nicholas heard an eerie, soft voice, speaking deliberately.

Nicholas opened the lid of the chest and looked at the coat.

"It is cold – put it on." This time the voice was louder – it sounded like Aemilia.

Nicholas reached into the chest and put on the dirty coat.

"Now help me, Nicholas. Help me." The voice was Aemilia's – she didn't speak with urgency or fear, but softly and purposefully.

"Where are you, Aemilia?"

"Down here. Below you."

Nicholas looked below him and began removing the floor of this second room. Again, he ripped up just enough boards, let himself down, and landed in a third room.

This room was dark – there was little light – certainly no light from the torches in the room above. Nicholas looked up – that room wasn't even there anymore. It was all just very dark.

"I'm over here, Nicholas. Help me." Aemilia called to him and Nicholas started walking toward the voice.

After a few steps, he could see her in the distance.

"I'm coming, Aemilia. I'm coming."

Nicholas started jogging toward her. As he got closer he saw that she was bound by ropes.

"Hold on, Aemilia! I'm coming!" Nicholas spoke with greater resolve. Now he began running toward her.

As he got closer, she was pulled farther from him.

"Hold on, Aemilia! I'm coming!" Nicholas yelled as he sprinted toward her.

Nicholas ran as fast as he could, but Aemilia kept getting farther and farther away.

"Help me, Nick! Help me, Nick! Help me, Nick!" Aemilia was screaming frantically – Nicholas had never seen her like that before.

"I'm coming, Aemilia! Hold on, I'm coming!"

Nicholas was running so quickly that he tripped and fell to his knees. Instead of hitting the ground, he fell and fell and fell. He kept dropping, as if through a long tunnel. He screamed as he fell and he flailed his arms and legs – sure he was about to die.

Suddenly, Nicholas was standing on a hard surface. Was this a fourth room? In some respects, it seemed like it, but Nicholas realized he was outside.

He heard a sound – a burning sound. As he turned behind him to see it, the intense heat warmed his cold face.

It was a fire. Not the barn, but the church! Nicholas could hear people inside the church, screaming in fear and pain.

Nicholas turned around and ran the other way – away from the church. As he ran, he tripped and fell over a beggar.

He looked into the man's hollow face – the man looked like a ghost or a demon. He got up, stumbling backwards as he tried to get away from the man.

As he turned around to continue running, he tripped over a second beggar. This one too had a hollow, ghostlike face.

Nicholas stood up and tried to start running again. Only now he was surrounded by beggars. He tried to move and they all reached out and grabbed him – some asking for money, some asking for food, some asking for help, and some asking for love.

Nicholas couldn't move and he felt suffocated by the mob of beggars. He shrunk to the ground, and a sea of people washed over him, as if he was drowning in an ocean of humanity.

*** *** *** *** *** *** *** *** *** *** ***

"Take it easy, buddy."
Nicholas cracked open his eyes. It was Rufus. Rufus was placing a wet cloth on Nicholas's head.
"I thought you might not make it. You had me pretty worried."
Nicholas was too weak to speak or to move. He scanned his environment with his eyes and realized he was in his father's cabin.
"Here, let me help you eat this. I made some soup. You need to get your strength back."
Rufus fed Nicholas a few bites of soup. Nicholas wasn't aware of much, but he could feel the warmth of the fresh soup circulating through his body. After those bites, he fell asleep and dreamed a second time.

*** *** *** *** *** *** *** *** *** *** ***

Nicholas was standing in Myra – outside of the orphanage that he passed on his way to the cabin. It was a larger building than Nicholas realized – he wondered how there could be that many orphan children in Myra.
Nicholas walked through the front door; it was a large wooden door. He didn't even think to knock, he just walked in as if he was supposed to go in. Inside he found a grand foyer. He saw Papa Antony off to the side in the foyer, but they didn't speak to each other – it was as if Papa Antony couldn't speak and as if Nicholas wasn't supposed to speak to him. There was hardly any light in the foyer; the only light came from an open door off to the right.

Nicholas walked toward the light. The room's door was only partly open, so when Nicholas reached it, he slowly pushed the door all the way open.

Inside the room he saw about a dozen children. They varied in age, maybe from four to 11. The children were happy and had bright, beautiful faces. They were laughing and talking and playing with toys. A few children sat over in the corner, playing a game together. The room not only looked happy, it felt happy. Nicholas felt warm while he was in the room. He could feel the joy. He could feel the happiness. He could feel their satisfaction.

Nicholas sensed that this was where he belonged. Somehow, he felt like this was his room – not his bedroom or not his house, but that he was the keeper of this room. These children were under his care.

But, after a moment in that room, the light began to fade. He felt the need to leave and backed out through the doorway and turned around. On the other side of the foyer, he saw a second room with a door slightly open and a light shining through its opening. Nicholas headed over toward the second room of the orphanage, curious what he would find when he opened its door.

Nicholas pushed open the door and took one step into the room. The light in this room was not as bright. Nicholas looked around the room and saw about a dozen beds, each with children either falling asleep or trying to fall asleep. There was a look of happiness and anticipation in their faces – even on the children who were asleep. Much like the last room, these children had expressions of joy and bright, beautiful faces. Nicholas could sense excitement in the room. Nicholas could sense anticipation in the room. Some of the children tossed and turned, not because they were uncomfortable, but because they were excited. Nicholas didn't know why, but he just knew they were excited – the way you know things in dreams even if no one tells you them.

Nicholas could feel that this room also belonged to a particular person, much like he was in charge of the last room. Nicholas didn't see an adult there, but he felt this room belonged to a man who was adventurous and carefree – a fun, passionate man who no doubt led these children on great adventures.

Like the last room, the already dim light in this room began to fade. Nicholas sensed that it was his time to leave the room, so he turned around and walked back through the door. He looked back at the first room and it was still dark, the door open just like he left it. Peering farther down the hall of the great foyer, Nicholas noticed for the first time a third room whose door was cracked with a light shining through it. So, Nicholas walked slowly toward the third door and gently pushed it open.

The light in this third room was much different than the light in the first two rooms. Nicholas could still see, but it was as if the light was black instead of white. In this room Nicholas heard crying, a soft crying. The site in this room was very sad and depressing. Like the last room, Nicholas saw about a dozen beds. But, these beds were full of sick children. Their faces were gray and they were afflicted by some type of disease, each of them on their own path to death.

There were two nurses wandering around the room, from bed to bed, trying to do what they could to help ease each child's pain. It was as if all they could do was treat the children's symptoms, trying to make their patients feel better instead of actually get better. Then, Nicholas heard someone speak. Over in the corner of the room was a person in the shadows, repeating over and over again, "Bring them back to life. Bring them back to life. Bring them back to life." The voice repeated the words, without emotion and without urgency.

Like the first two rooms, Nicholas could feel that this room also had a person in charge. It wasn't the nurses or the owner of the voice in the corner of the room. Like the last room, Nicholas never saw this person in charge, but could sense that it was a woman. She had a difficult life and was fiercely independent and scarred by her experiences.

Nicholas was uncomfortable in this room, but he could not find it in himself to turn around and leave. Then, thankfully the bland light in this room dimmed as the lights had in the last two rooms, and Nicholas was released to turn around and walk back through the door.

Experiencing the third room made Nicholas want to leave the orphanage, but he was compelled to stay. Looking farther down the hall, he saw a fourth and final room. He could tell it was the final room, because the hallway ended at this room. Like the third room, a faint yet somehow blackish light shone through the cracked door. Everything in Nicholas wanted to turn around and leave, but he walked toward the room anyway.

Nicholas opened the door and saw a sight worse than dying children. This room was full of children without faces. Nicholas was overwhelmed by a sense of lostness and hopelessness. No one spoke and no one moved – they just stood there, looking miserable. It was if Nicholas was in a room of Hades itself, full of former spirits of forgotten children. In fact, Nicholas could tell that this room did not even have an adult overseer like the other three rooms did.

This room had a profound emotional impact on Nicholas. He started to softly cry, but that soon turned into a steady stream of tears. Before long Nicholas was crying uncontrollably – he so identified with the sense of emptiness and loneliness these small, lifeless, faceless figures were enduring, but for the first time in months, his emotions were overcome with compassion for someone else and not for himself.

Nicholas experienced a euphoric empathy for these children, unexplainable by words. Nicholas fell to his knees, continuing to cry. He cried out to God, speaking for the first time in the orphanage, "God, what can be done? What can be done?"

While Nicholas was sobbing, someone tapped on his shoulder. He looked up and saw a little girl. This girl had a face, unlike the children in this room. She was not grey with sickness, but she also was not full of brightness like the children in the first two rooms. She had both a sense of familiarity and unfamiliarity to Nicholas, as if he knew her and didn't know her at the same time.

"Will you help us?" she asked.

Nicholas looked at her for a moment and then whispered, "What can I do?"

"Will you help us?" she asked again.

"But I have nothing. I am nothing. What can I do?"

Unfazed, the little girl peered deeply into Nicholas's eyes as if she could see into his soul. She asked a third time, "Will you help us, Nicholas?"

"Yes," Nicholas said confidently. Then he whispered again, "Yes."

*** *** *** *** *** *** *** *** *** *** ***

Nicholas woke up from his sleep, feeling rested and renewed, with tears gently wandering down his face. Whatever soup Rufus gave him did the trick. He was warm and his head no longer hurt.

He didn't tell Rufus he was awake. He lay on the bed, still as he could be, thinking about his two dreams. He felt different. He was confused, but felt like he had more clarity than any other time during the last three months.

His mind raced with so many emotions – the warmth of the children playing and the chill of the faceless children. The girl asking him for help. The voice of his parents. Aemilia needing rescued, but not being able to do it. That silly coat. The anticipation of the children in the beds. The church burning.

His eyes darted above him as he thought about the dreams. The dreams left him feeling very different – like someone had reset his entire existence. He no longer doubted there was a God and his mind wasn't even racing through "Why?" questions about his parents' death or his loneliness or his loss of wealth and business. He started asking "What?"

questions. What was his purpose? What does God want to do with all of this? What can he do to help those children?

Then, in the peace of his bed and with his questions unanswered, Nicholas closed his eyes and prayed in his head, "God, please forgive me. I believe you and in you. I'm so sorry."

Nicholas felt the warmth of his soul match the warmth that his body felt from Rufus's soup.

Nicholas kept his eyes closed for a moment and then slowly reopened his eyes. He experienced a peace he hadn't felt in months. The room was lit only by Rufus's fire. Off to the side, he could see a shelf hanging on the wall. There were a couple of jars, a few bags, and something that was glimmering in the light. His eyes fixated on that glimmering object. What was it? It had a dull shine that made it seem a bit more vibrant than anything else on the shelf.

Nicholas slowly sat up, which completely startled Rufus.

"Hey, you look a lot better, my friend! I bet you're hungry." Rufus grabbed some more soup and went over to Nicholas, ready to continue nursing his friend back to health.

"Hey, Rufus. I am hungry." Nicholas didn't look at Rufus, but kept looking toward the glimmer, trying to figure out what it was – something drew him to it. He didn't even think about why his friend was in his father's cabin and how they both got there.

"OK, buddy, I have some soup right here." Rufus started to feed Nicholas, but Nicholas turned his eyes toward Rufus, smiled, and gently took the spoon to feed himself.

"I'm glad you're feeling better. After I left your house, I took a walk around the block and decided to go back, except you weren't there. I looked all over for you and about gave up. On my way home, I passed a beggar who was buying an apple. I made a comment to him, congratulating him on having a little bit of money. He told me that a guy, who sounded a lot like you, tossed him a coin and headed out of town. I knew it was you and I knew you were coming here. Except, imagine how surprised I was when I found you about 500 yards from here, lying flat on the snow. I thought you were dead, but you weren't and I did my best to get you here."

"I don't know how I can ever thank you, Rufus," Nicholas said, as he devoured the soup. "I'm so sorry for how I acted. I was a real idiot."

"That's OK, Nick. You've been through a lot. Just know that I'm here to help you."

"Thanks, Rufus."

Nicholas ate a few more bites of soup and then he remembered the strange object on the shelf.

"Hey Rufus, can you get something down for me?"

"Sure"

"Up on that shelf, there's something shiny. Will you get it down?"

Rufus walked over to the shelf, slid a couple of jars to the side, and reached up, pulling the object down.

"It's jewelry of some sort."

As Rufus handed the jewelry to Nicholas, Nicholas saw that it was his father's gold necklace – the Christian necklace that was passed down from father to father to father, the very necklace Nicholas was looking for in the barn.

Without saying a word, Nicholas began to cry. Rufus, at first confused, started to talk, "Oh! That's the…" He didn't even finish his sentence.

Nicholas was weeping while he spoke. "Rufus, I've been such a fool! All this time God has loved me and cared for me. He blessed my life way beyond anything I could ever deserve and when I lost a bit of it, I got so mad."

Nicholas wept and Rufus even started crying. Nicholas took the necklace and put it on. It felt like the necklace belonged on him.

9 – The Return

Nicholas and Rufus decided that they would spend that night, Friday night, at the cabin and then head down the mountain the next morning. Nicholas had a renewed sense of purpose, though he didn't really have a plan of what he was going to do when he got home.

They spent the evening going through the cabin. It wasn't a big cabin, basically just one big room. There were shelves and chests full of various items – mostly blankets, cooking utensils, and such. However, everything they found wasn't ordinary.

"Hey Rufus, can you reach those large bags up on that shelf? The ones that were beside the necklace?"

Rufus reached up and tried to get one down with a single hand. "Whoa! This is heavy!" Rufus reevaluated his one-handed decision and grabbed a chair to stand on while using both hands to get the first bag down.

"Here you go," he said as he plopped the bag on the bed Nicholas was sitting on.

Nicholas opened the bag and could hardly believe his eyes.

"This bag is full of coins!" Nicholas exclaimed. "And not just denarii, but a bunch of different kinds of coins! There must be 25,000 denarii in this bag alone!"

"No way, Nick! Let me grab the other bag!"

Sure enough, the second bag had as much money in it as the first bag.

"This must be why the third hole was empty at the barn!" Nicholas surmised.

And, just like that, Nicholas went from hopeless and broke to full of purpose and quite wealthy. Of course, it is no coincidence that he found his new purpose before he found his new wealth.

"Wow! I just can't believe that my dad brought all of this money up here."

"It's a good thing he did, with the fire and all."

"Yeah, I suppose so."

With Nicholas's spirits renewed by both his re-found faith in God and the undying faithfulness of his friend Rufus, finding the necklace and money were just icing on the cake. The two men spent the rest of the evening remembering adventures from their childhood, talking about Nicholas's parents, and dreaming aloud about the future. Nicholas felt truly blessed to be in this moment and, for the first time since his parents' death, he felt like he was actually on the path toward healing and moving forward with his life.

*** *** *** *** *** *** *** *** *** *** ***

Saturday morning Nicholas and Rufus rose early, ate a breakfast of Rufus's restorative soup, grabbed some coins and started their trip down the mountain. They could only easily carry about 5,000 denarii between the two of them. The coins were pretty heavy and they knew it would be best not to overdo it for the long journey home – especially since Nicholas had just been in such poor health. Nicholas, however, felt much better after a good night's sleep, and it helped that he was in a much better state of mind. Besides Nicholas's health inhibiting their ability to carry many coins, the ground was muddy from the snow and they didn't have a cart or anything to help bring more money down the mountain.

The trip down the mountain typically only takes about two-thirds of the time that it takes to get up the mountain. And, even with a heavy bag of coins, this trip was no exception. Nicholas and Rufus arrived in Myra by midafternoon – the sun was shining and the weather was much warmer. Because of the warm weather, the town was quite active.

Soon after they entered town, Nicholas and Rufus passed by the orphanage. It didn't look like it did in his dream, but Nicholas understood that it was the same place. There were two children playing outside the orphanage, chasing each other and having a good time.

"Hey, you! Come here." Nicholas motioned to the two orphans and they walked slowly toward him, smiles erased from their faces and looking down at the ground. It wasn't usually a good thing when a strange adult called over a pair of orphans.

"What are your names?"

"I'm Kristopher," spoke the taller and likely older boy. He must have been seven or eight years old.

"And I'm Denys," spoke the second child, a little softer but slightly emboldened by the other boy speaking up first.

"Well, my name is Nicholas and I want you to have this." Nicholas reached into his bag and pulled out two coins – he didn't even know which two kinds of coins he grabbed. He placed one coin in each boy's hand.

Their smiles reached as far across their faces as possible.

"Thanks, sir," Kristopher spoke, quickly followed by Denys.

"Not a problem, boys. Now go back and keep playing!"

Nicholas looked at Rufus, smiled, and then resumed his walk through town. Rufus was proud of his friend – he certainly could tell that there was something different about Nicholas.

A few minutes later Nicholas saw a beggar in the distance, kind of out of the way and partially down a side street. Nicholas slowed down and studied the man intently. He was certain it was the same man he had seen with Aemilia a few months ago and the same man to whom he sarcastically tossed a coin a couple of days ago as he escaped out of Myra.

For the first time Nicholas noticed the wrinkles in the beggar's face. He wore a face of hardship and sun – probably spending much of his life outside. He noticed that the beggar had a leg deformity. He couldn't walk well if he tried, which is probably why Nicholas always saw him sitting down.

Nicholas told Rufus that he wanted to go talk to the man and they crossed the street to head toward him. As they got near, Nicholas saw that his clothes had rips and holes, and that he held a small bag with its own rips. Coming upon the man, Nicholas smelled him for the first time – he smelled like his only baths were the rains that fell mostly in the winter.

However, when Nicholas approached the man, he found that his appearance and smell did not matter. He looked at the man directly in the eyes, almost like Nicholas had the power to see past the man's outer appearance and into his heart. In a brief moment of Déjà vu, Nicholas remembered the little girl in the fourth room of his dream who looked so deeply into his eyes – almost as if she were looking right into his soul. Nicholas saw the man for who he was – a human needing compassion.

"My name is Nicholas." The man didn't respond.

"I want you to know that I am not special and I have been a very self-centered, poor man. Poor in spirit and poor in love." With that unrehearsed speech said, Nicholas reached into his bag and extended toward the man a handful of coins. He must have pulled out 250 denarii.

"I want you to have this. Please have peace in your life."

The man sat dumbfounded. Nicholas couldn't tell if the man could even speak or understand what he was saying. However, the man opened his hands and Nicholas dropped the coins in his hands – several of them spilling over and landing on the ground. The man's eyes began to water, and Nicholas and Rufus continued on their way.

They arrived at Nicholas's house a little bit later. Nicholas was so happy to be home that he didn't even notice the parchment that was nailed to his door. Nicholas thanked his friend for his help and tried to send Rufus home with a bit of money. Rufus wouldn't take it though, and Nicholas gave him a hug as Rufus went out the door.

Nicholas looked around the house. It didn't feel lonely like it had before, but it did have a feeling of emptiness like the emptiness that comes when you realize something isn't as important as you once thought it was. He was grateful for the house, but he had a much different perspective now.

It was starting to get dark, so Nicholas decided that he should spend the evening cleaning up the filthy mess he created over the previous three months. Tomorrow would be Sunday – he planned to go to church and then after that, to go find Aemilia. He had a lot he wanted to say to her, if she would even be willing to hear him speak at all. He played his potential conversations with her over and over in his head as he cleaned his house. Of course, he still did not know about Aemilia's family's dire situation.

That night Nicholas slept in his bed and he slept more soundly than he had slept since his parents died. He had a profound peace, a proper perspective, and a renewed purpose for life.

*** *** *** *** *** *** *** *** *** *** ***

The next morning Nicholas rose early. The birds were singing and the sun was shining. Being Sunday, he planned to not only go to church, but to actually get there early for a change.

He left his much cleaner house with a spring in his step. His newfound purpose in life overshadowed the little bit of nerves he had about talking to Aemilia later today. He even found himself whistling as he walked down the road to church.

As he got close enough to see the church, he was relieved to see that the building looked just fine, despite it being on fire in his dream. He actually hadn't been to church since his parents died. Papa Antony visited him from time to time, but Nicholas was usually cold toward him and did what he could do to get him to leave.

Nicholas was the first to arrive to church – even before Papa Antony. He remembered that during the colder months there was often a fire in the fireplace, so Nicholas took it upon himself to start the fire.

The church building was a simple building – mostly one large room with several benches lined up in rows. At the front of the church was a podium where Papa Antony would deliver his sermon. The fireplace was off to the left side. When it was particularly cold, most of the congregation sat on that side to be near the fire. There were just a few churches in Myra. Aemilia and her family attended one of the other churches.

A few minutes after the fire was going well, Papa Antony arrived.

"Nicholas, it is so good to see you. You are actually about the last person I expected to be here when I saw the smoke rising through the chimney a moment ago."

"Well, Papa Antony, I've had a bit of a moment, I suppose. I had a moment of clarity, where I realized that everything is going to be OK and that God still is here. I've been so selfish and wrapped up in my own world. I think I see things much clearer now."

"That's so good to hear, Nicholas. You have certainly had a lot to go through. And now, I hear that things seem to have gotten worse for you. It is refreshing to see you trusting in God and with a smile on your face."

"Thanks, Papa Antony. I feel better and I am better."

Instead of recounting his trip to the cabin, his dreams, and finding the necklace and money, Nicholas instead asked Papa Antony questions about Papa Antony's life. He realized that Papa Antony spent so much of his life giving to other people. Nicholas felt bad that he had known Papa Antony for so long, but had never even known where Papa Antony was from or how he became a priest.

A little bit later, members of the congregation began to arrive for the morning's service. Most of them warmly greeted Nicholas, genuinely happy that he was back in church. More than one person joked with Nicholas about his being to church on time for a change.

Nicholas sat through the church service, paying attention more intently than he ever had before. He not only sang the songs with vigor and purpose, but he also listened to the words that he was singing and allowed them to penetrate deeply within him.

When it came time to collect an offering, Nicholas gladly reached into his pocket and placed a handful of coins in the plate. Most people were surprised that he had any money to give – word had traveled quickly that Alexander was the owner of all of Nicholas's money.

During the sermon, Nicholas felt a connection to the scripture like he had never felt before. Papa Antony preached about Abraham's obedience to follow God to a new land. In the story, God called Abraham to leave his culture, his home country, and his family, and to go to a place that God would show him when he arrived. Abraham obeyed and made the trek across the Fertile Crescent to what would become Israel. As a result of his obedience, God blessed Abraham with seven promises, the most important being that all nations on earth would be blessed through him.

Nicholas's heart was pricked throughout the sermon. "Maybe God is calling me," he thought. "Maybe there is something to all the times people said that I should be a priest. Perhaps they saw something that I couldn't see."

At the end of the service, Nicholas hung around to talk with Papa Antony. He did have his plan to speak with Aemilia, but he felt like this was important and he didn't want to wait until next Sunday to speak with Papa Antony.

"Papa Antony, how did you know that you were supposed to be a priest?"

"Well Nicholas, in my case it was as if God had aligned everything in my life toward that end. The things people told me, the tugs on my heart, the dissatisfaction I had with what I planned to do with my life, even my reading of scripture. All of those things pointed toward the priesthood."

"Was there a moment, a time when you knew without a doubt that you should be a priest?"

"I don't know about a particular moment. I suppose I can say that God had been working on my heart for some time. One morning Papa Thomas, the priest where I attended church, asked me to lead a portion of the church service. It was only a minor role, but it felt so right. I suppose that it was at that moment that I knew I should become a priest. However, figuring it out in my heart and then having the obedience to go through with it didn't happen at the same time. It took me a good six months after I felt sure before I finally surrendered and decided to follow through with it. Why do you ask, Nicholas?"

"I don't know. I just know that things are really different now. I feel like there is so much more to my life than I understand – like there is a much bigger purpose to the world and to life in general. I don't know if that means I should be a priest, but there's something there and I can't quite put my finger on it."

"Well, Nicholas, give it time. You don't have to have all of the answers today. If God wants you to be a priest, then he isn't going to forget about it quite so easily. It will either make more sense or it will pass."

"Thank you, Papa Antony. I think I needed to hear that to have the freedom to let this run its course."

"No problem, Nicholas. Now tell me, what are your plans this afternoon? And, where are you staying?"

Nicholas was a little confused by Papa Antony's second question, but decided to answer his first question. "This afternoon I plan to go find a friend. I spoke pretty harshly to her a few days ago. In fact, I've been pretty bad to her over the last few months. I don't know if she even wants to talk to me or even cares, but I feel like I've got to try. At the very least I can apologize. If she doesn't see it as genuine or if she doesn't care, then I suppose I deserve it."

Papa Antony didn't really know Aemilia and her family. After all, they attended a different church in town. Of course, he met her, and particularly her mother, Faustina, when they were planning Nicholas's parents' funeral. However, the talk of the town was Alexander's demand of money from Stephen and how he was about to lose his daughters. Papa Antony did not even figure out that Nicholas was talking about Aemilia. If so, then he would have let Nicholas know what was happening to her and her family.

"OK, Nicholas. It is always good to try and restore friendships. Now my other question, where are you staying?"

"What do you mean, 'Where are you staying?' I am staying in my house."

"Your house? I was pretty sure that you didn't have a house anymore?"

"What are you talking about?"

"The talk around town is that you were supposed to pay Alexander 4,000 aurei and that you also signed over your half of the business. Alexander and some banker counted the money and it was 100 aurei short. In kind of a rush decision, the magistrate ordered that Alexander got your house to settle the debt. Isn't that true?"

"No, I stayed in my house last night."

Both men were puzzled, standing silently for a few seconds.

"But, I didn't stay there the previous two nights before that. Maybe something happened when I was at my father's cabin in the mountains."

Papa Antony's face lengthened, realizing that this wasn't the first time he had to break bad news to Nicholas. "Nicholas, my son, I am afraid you have lost your house. I am certain it has been decreed. Let me walk with you to the magistrate and see what we can find out. I've never trusted that Alexander. He is not a kind man."

Nicholas looked at him in silence, calmly processing what Papa Antony was saying.

"No, that's OK. Thank you. I can do it on my own." Nicholas paused. "You know, I never counted the money. I just hoped there was enough there."

Nicholas was a little confused and a little in shock, but his perspective wasn't changed. "I can handle this one too," he thought, as he started walking back to what he had recently thought was his house.

A few minutes later, he arrived in his courtyard. Neptune was lying in the corner and didn't bother to get up. Three months of neglect led Neptune to not expect anything when he saw Nicholas.

As Nicholas neared his front door, he saw the posted parchment that he had missed in the dimness of the night before. It was a notice – the house was Alexander's house. The house he grew up in, practically the only possession he was left with in Myra, the house he slept in last night – it wasn't his.

Nicholas sat down on the ground outside the door, calling Neptune to his side. He would have to get some things out of the house – maybe he could stay with Rufus while he figured things out. But that would have to wait for now. As important as his house was and as much as he needed to get his newfound money out of the house, his friendship, or rather his love, with Aemilia was more important. "The house will have to wait," he thought. And he picked himself up, attached a leash that he found in the courtyard to Neptune, and they both walked to Aemilia's house.

10 – Trouble

As Nicholas walked the short walk to Aemilia's house he thought about Alexander.

"I just can't believe that Alexander took my house. I really thought he had my best interests in mind."

He wrestled with these thoughts. On the one hand he justified that Alexander was simply doing what was right – after all Nicholas did owe him 4,000 aurei and he apparently didn't give him enough money. Perhaps Alexander really had to have the money as soon as possible to pay off debts and to try to keep the business afloat. Nicholas reasoned that perhaps Alexander was just doing what he had to do and that he didn't really want to take Nicholas's house.

On the other hand, the seed of doubt that Papa Antony placed in Nicholas's head – that Alexander was not to be trusted – was starting to find its roots. Nicholas thought back to various dealings he had with Alexander over the years. Nicholas thought about the ways that Alexander dealt with his parents – having them spend their money and host the parties. Nicholas thought it odd that Alexander was always the person with the business contacts and the next best deal.

"Maybe he's not a good person after all," Nicholas thought.

When he turned the corner and saw Aemilia's house in the distance, he suddenly snapped out of thinking about Alexander and remembered that he was about to attempt to talk to Aemilia.

Would she forgive him? Would she still want to be friends? Is there still a possibility that there is more to their relationship than friendship? Would she even be willing to talk with him at all?

Nicholas approached the house. It was a beautiful December day. The sun was shining and the air was blowing off the sea, wafting a slight, salty scent through the air. Nicholas knocked on the door. His knock sounded foreign to him – he couldn't remember the last time he knocked on a door.

No answer.

Nicholas waited, somewhat eagerly and impatiently. He knocked again.

Still no answer.

A next-door neighbor opened up her door. She must have been rich, since she lived in this neighborhood, but her face was stained by the stress of life. She wore her emotions on her face, and her face said that she wasn't an easy person to be around. "What do you want?" she asked rudely.

"I'm a friend of Aemilia's – I've come to talk to her. Do you know, is anyone home?"

"They aren't here. They haven't been here since this morning. Now I suggest you turn around and go back the way you came."

Nicholas had been to Aemilia's house plenty of times, but this lady seemed unfamiliar. He studied her for a second, and then it dawned on him – she was his mom's old friend, Alexia.

"Alexia, it's me, Nicholas – Johanna's son."

"Nicky, is that you? Oh my, I haven't seen you in years. You look so much older now." Her mood changed and her face softened when she realized who he was. "Oh, Nicky, I'm so sorry about your parents. I just can't imagine. How are you doing?"

"Thank you. It has been difficult, but I'm doing much better now. So, do you know where Aemilia is?"

When Nicholas reminded her why he was there, her face soured again – this time more of a sad face than an angry face.

"I'm not quite sure, Nicky. I'll tell you what, I'll let her know you stopped by. Where will you be? Do you want her to come to you later?"

"Uh, I'm not quite sure. Tell her that I'll be back tonight, before sunset."

"OK, no problem, Nicky."

"Thanks, Alexia."

"Sure, honey. I'll see you around."

Nicholas turned around and he and Neptune left Aemilia's house, disappointed that he would have to wait longer to know her response to him.

Nicholas decided to stop by his house and get his money. Or, at least, his old house. He figured he would carry the bag to Rufus's house – it was the best place he could think of to spend the night. It would be awkward to ask Aemilia's family if he could stay there – he might not exactly be welcome. He was sure that Rufus's parents would let him stay there, at least for a few nights. If that failed, then he could probably ask Papa Antony, who would either let Nicholas stay with him or find someone in the church who would let Nicholas stay with them.

"It is kind of ironic," Nicholas thought, "I have more money than I could possibly need in one lifetime and yet I don't have a place to stay." It's interesting how something that normally has so much value means very little when we actually prioritize things. Ask a wanderer in the desert who hasn't had a drink of water in two days what they would choose between a flask of water and a month's wages, and he will choose the water every time. Ask a lonely, rich man on his deathbed if he would trade all of the money that made him rich for fulfilling relationships and loved ones to pass on his legacy, and he will choose the people every time.

As Nicholas passed through the center of town, he passed by the Court of Records. This large, Roman building had a posting area outside where legal notices were placed for the public to see. Nicholas decided to stop by and take a look – there were only about a dozen posts.

After skimming through the first two posts, he saw a post about his house. "The court grants Alexander of Myra the deed to the house of Nicholas of Myra (formerly the house of Epiphanius of Myra) in lieu of all outstanding debts that Nicholas of Myra owes Alexander of Myra. All debts are now paid in full."

"At least that is the end of it," Nicholas mumbled under his breath. "There's nothing else I owe to Alexander. And, he doesn't know about the money from my dad's cabin. So, as far as he knows, I don't have anything else left to give."

The very next post also bore Nicholas's name. "The court now recognizes that the entire textile and linen business, formerly partly owned by Nicholas of Myra (and before that, Epiphanius of Myra), now belongs fully to Alexander of Myra. This includes all assets and all debts."

"Well, he can have it," Nicholas was again mumbling to himself.

Nicholas figured that was the last post that had to do with him or Alexander, so he shot a cursory glance over the rest of the posts as he picked up his bags to walk on to Rufus's house. As he took one step away, he froze in his steps when he ran across the names "Stephen and Faustina."

"What is this?" Nicholas wondered, setting his bags back down.

"The court recognizes that Stephen and Faustina of Myra have until Tuesday morning to pay Alexander of Myra 5,000 denarii, Wednesday morning another 5,000 denarii, and Thursday morning a third 5,000 denarii. If the debtors cannot pay their debts by the appointed time, then the creditor has the freedom to exercise his rights under Roman law."

Nicholas's mind raced. "5,000 denarii by Tuesday? 15,000 denarii in total? Why? Why would they owe Alexander so much money? And what happens if they don't pay? What are Alexander's rights under Roman law?"

Nicholas picked up his bags again and walked toward Rufus's house, troubled by what he just read.

"Alexander doesn't even know Stephen and Faustina that well," he thought. "Why would they owe him so much money?

"Maybe this is my fault. Has Alexander's coming after me and my money affected Aemilia's family? Certainly not.

"Rights under Roman law? What could that mean? Can Alexander take their house like he took mine? Is their house worth 15,000 denarii? Will he take their business as well?"

Nicholas's racing mind made the walk to Rufus's house pass quickly.

Nicholas arrived at Rufus's house. Calling it a house might be too generous – it was really part of a large apartment building. Rufus, his parents, and his four younger siblings (Rufus had three older siblings who had already moved out on their own), all lived in the second floor of a building that seemed to stretch forever. Most of the people in this part of town lived in buildings that were two or three stories high with outside steps leading up to each of the residences. These buildings were very big and often took up entire city blocks. The apartments were small and cramped (especially for a family of seven!), with not much more than a place to sleep and eat.

Rufus's mother, Agnes, was proud of her home. Though it wasn't much, she worked hard to keep it clean – you would never guess that so many children lived in the house because it always looked so neat.

Nicholas climbed the stairway to Rufus's apartment. Nicholas would have practiced his door knocking for the second time today, but the door was already open. He peeked his head in, and called out.

"Is anyone home?"

Agnes looked up from cleaning a pot. "Nicholas! How are you doing, son? Are you hungry?" She was always so kind to Nicholas and always offered him food. He was amazed that someone with so many mouths to feed would be so generous and willing to feed him. Rufus's dad was always polite to Nicholas too, but he felt that it always seemed a little fake, like Rufus's dad knew that Nicholas had money and Nicholas's father could give him work. In fact, Nicholas had seen Rufus's dad have quite a temper with Rufus.

"I'm well. Thank you."

"Well, Rufus is around here somewhere." She turned to the side and yelled, "Rufus! Nicholas is here!" Turning back to Nicholas she said, "So, how are you getting along, son? Rufus said that he and you went up to your cabin for a couple of days."

"Yes, Rufus was a good friend to me. Hey listen, what I came to ask Rufus really needs to be asked of you. Can Neptune and I stay here for a few nights?"

"Of course, dear. Is your big house getting too lonely for you?" Agnes didn't mean to compare her apartment to Nicholas's house, it was just the way she was.

"No, ma'am. My big house isn't my big house anymore. I lost it."

"Whatever do you mean, you lost it?"

"I owed my dad's business partner, Alexander, a lot of money. I didn't have it, so the house went to him."

"I never have trusted that man, Alexander. I tell you what, I always told Rufus's dad, 'Don't work for that Alexander. You can't trust him. He'll do you wrong!'"

"I'm beginning to see that, ma'am."

Rufus skipped up the stairs to his front door and bolted through.

"Hey, Nick. What brings you to my side of town?"

"I need a place to stay, Rufus. Alexander took my house."

"What? What do you mean? How could he do that?"

"I owed him a lot of money and apparently I didn't have it. So, the court gave him my house as the rest of the payment."

"Well you have money now, don't you? Just go back and buy the house."

"I doubt it'd be that easy, Rufus. And besides, Alexander would probably charge me double!" Nicholas laughed as he talked. His demeanor had come a long way in the last few days. Now something as big as losing his house seemed trivial.

"And," Nicholas continued, "I don't really want Alexander to know I have any money. I'm sure he'd hatch up some scheme to get the rest of it from me too."

"Well, you're welcome to stay here, Nicholas," Agnes interjected. "Stay as long as you like."

"Thank you, ma'am." Then Nicholas turned to Rufus. "Hey Rufus, can we go talk somewhere?"

"Absolutely, buddy." Rufus kissed his mother on the cheek and Nicholas and Rufus headed down the stairs and onto the street. After walking a minute, they found a bench and sat down and talked.

"Rufus, do you know what's going on with Aemilia's family?"

"I don't know what you're talking about, Nicholas? I haven't seen Aemilia in a long time. I don't think I've really talked to her since we all went to the barn a few months ago." Rufus paused. "Well, actually, I did see her one day when we both went to your house about a month ago. You didn't want to see either one of us on that day and I happened to arrive at your house when she was leaving. She was pretty upset. We talked for a minute – it was about nothing, really – and then she went on her way. Well, actually I walked her home. Why, what do you mean, 'What's going with Aemilia's family?'"

"I passed by the Court of Records this afternoon and saw the judgments posted. I saw the judgment about my house and how I gave Alexander the business."

"He *took* your house and business," Rufus interrupted. "At least that's the way I see it. He stole them from you."

"Well, maybe so, but I gave him the money and signed over the business, so I don't know if that can count as thievery."

"It counts as thievery in my book! So, what about Aemilia?"

"Oh yeah. So, I was looking at the posts and I saw a post that said something about Aemilia's parents, 'Stephen and Faustina of Myra,' owing 'Alexander of Myra' '15,000 denarii.' And there was something about Alexander could 'exercise his rights under Roman law' if they didn't pay."

"Wow, I hadn't heard a thing. It must be a business debt or something."

"Yeah, I don't know. I do know that the first 5,000 denarii is due in two days – Tuesday morning. I am half-tempted to just go pay it all off myself. I don't even care about money anymore."

"Huh, well who knows what the debt is for, Nick. Chances are if you paid it off then Alexander would come after both you and them for something else. Before long, you wouldn't have any money and Aemilia's parents would still be in trouble."

"Yeah, who knows. Anyway, hopefully I'll find out soon. I'm going to go back to Aemilia's house to try to talk to her. I stopped by her house earlier, but she wasn't home. I talked to her neighbor who said they hadn't been home since this morning. I told her that if she saw Aemilia, to let her know that I would be stopping by again this evening. I sure hope she talks to me. Before I wanted to talk to her just to apologize, but now I'm concerned for her and her family." Nicholas looked up at the sun, trying to determine how late in the day it was. "Actually, I probably better head there now."

"Do you need backup, buddy?"

"Ha! No, I need to handle this one on my own."

"Good luck!"

"Thanks."

*** *** *** *** *** *** *** *** *** *** ***

Leaving the coins and Neptune at Rufus's house, Nicholas walked the half-hour walk to Aemilia's house at a fairly brisk pace. His concern for how she would accept him was replaced by concern for her welfare. He was worried that her family would lose their house or their business. He didn't want to see Aemilia, her sisters, or her parents homeless and without anything (though for a moment he chuckled at the idea of Diantha being homeless).

Just as it happened earlier in the day, when Nicholas turned the corner and saw Aemilia's house his thoughts immediately re-centered on the task at hand. He needed to apologize to Aemilia and he was worried that she would not accept it. He was afraid that one of her sisters would answer the door – probably Diantha – and send him away, telling him that he didn't deserve her sister and that he could never see her again.

For the second time that day, Nicholas presented his newly minted knock on Aemilia's door. Stephen, looking sullen and stressed, opened the door.

"Oh hi, Nicholas. Alexia said you stopped by earlier. I'll get Aemilia."

"I'm here, daddy," Aemilia said as she peeked around the corner of the living room. "Is it OK if I go outside and talk to Nicholas?"

"I suppose, dear. Stay close to home – don't go anywhere."

"OK."

Nicholas couldn't believe it. Aemilia was willingly coming out of the house to talk with him. There were no overprotective sisters and Stephen wasn't shooing him away.

The pair walked a few steps from the door and sat down on a stone wall that ran through the neighborhood.

"Aemilia," Nicholas spoke first, "I really need to…"

"Oh, Nick!" Aemilia cut him off and buried herself into his arms. "Nick, it's so good to see you! I'm so scared."

"Scared? There's nothing to be scared of." Nicholas spoke quickly, thinking she was speaking about him. "I'm a lot better. I feel better and I went to the cabin and I almost died."

He paused for a second, realizing that telling her he almost died wouldn't make her not be scared. "Uh, don't worry, I'm fine now. Anyway, I had these weird dreams – I had them after I collapsed and Rufus found me and carried me to the cabin."

Nicholas paused again, realizing a second time that his story probably wasn't helping Aemilia feel better. "Then I realized how silly it all was and how God loves me and is in control." Nicholas took a deep breath and slowed down. "And well, I'm sorry. Sorry for how I treated you. Sorry I've been so selfish."

"Oh Nick. It's OK," Aemilia was crying as he spoke, but she didn't look relieved. Nicholas had played out this moment many times in his head over the last two days. In all of his best dreamed-up scenarios where she proclaimed "It's OK," he never once envisioned her face still looking troubled.

"That's good to hear, Aemilia. Thank you, but I think something else is wrong. Is everything OK?"

"No, Nicholas, it's terrible."

For the next few minutes, Aemilia recounted to Nicholas the events of the last week and a half. She told him about her father's arrest for his faith (this made Nicholas angry) and then how Alexander paid his fine (this made Nicholas angrier). Then she told him how that her father couldn't pay the money on time and that no one would help him or do business with him. Nicholas immediately suspected Alexander was at work in that too. Then she told him that Alexander had to have the payments beginning in two days or else she and her sisters would be sold as slaves.

In all of Nicholas's emotions of the past months, nothing quite compared to the sick feeling he felt when Aemilia gave him the news that she might become a slave. Like a contemporary biblical Job, Nicholas figured that in losing his parents, losing his money, and losing his house, he was ultimately redeemed by passing through the refiner's fire and finding his faith, finding his money, and refinding his girl. But, the obstacles in his life that he had finally conquered paled in comparison to the possibility of losing Aemilia to slavery. His personal story of redemption seemed to matter very little to him in this moment.

In a matter of seconds, he determined that he would pay the money and that would put an end to it. Who cares if Alexander found out he had more money? He would gladly give it all up to save Aemilia and her sisters.

"I'll pay the fine," Nicholas confidently declared.

"It's not that easy," Aemilia said. "The law says that no one can pay it for my father – it has to be his own money. And I'm afraid that Alexander has made sure that my father hasn't been able to get the money and also made sure that no one will be able to pay it for him."

"Well, he can't control everything. Certainly, your father has been able to get some money. How should Alexander know that he hasn't been able to get it all?"

"I'm certain Alexander knows we don't have it all. In fact, I heard my dad pleading with him last night – Alexander came by, I think just to rub it in."

"That man is so evil. It just burns me up inside." Nicholas was filled with rage.

"There's got to be a way I can help," Nicholas said, a little more calmly, but full of determination. "We have to come up with a plan – there must be a way."

"Nick, how can you help? I heard that you don't have any money left."

"I found money at the cabin – a lot of it. I'll give you everything you need."

"Nick, I can't ask you to pay that much money! You've already lost so much, and anyway, no one can pay the fine for us."

"Aemilia, it's not even a question you have to ask me. I'll do it in a heartbeat. I'll find a way – no one has to know it was me."

"But you've lost your business and your house. You need that money."

"I have way more money than I'll ever need – there isn't any reason to talk about it. I'll pay the 15,000 denarii."

Aemilia reached over, gave Nicholas a big hug, and began crying. She couldn't believe that just a few minutes ago she was sure she had lost both the man she might love and her entire future, and now everything seemed so bright and hopeful.

Nicholas held her in his arms. He whispered, "It's OK Aemilia. I would spend 15,000 denarii a million times over for you. I thought I lost you forever."

"You never lost me," she whispered back.

Aemilia looked up at Nicholas. For perhaps the first time in the entire conversation, they looked at each other in the eyes, intently fixing their gazes upon each other. After a pause of a few seconds, they slowly leaned their heads toward each other, closed their eyes, and kissed their first kiss – barely a pressing together of their previously untouched lips. It was a kiss that might be laughable by most standards, but in this moment, with these two young lovers, it was pure and perfect.

After the kiss they backed off from each other, noses just an inch apart. Neither of them quite knew what to say and neither of them quite knew what it meant.

Nicholas broke the awkwardness by turning back to the matter at hand. "We need a plan of how I'm going to get you the money. And, I only have 5,000 denarii at Rufus's house – the rest is at my father's cabin."

Nicholas and Aemilia talked about different ways for him to get her the money. Every plan they came up with required him to travel to and from his father's cabin by himself, which meant carrying a lot coins by himself.

At first they decided that Nicholas could just run to Rufus's house right now and then bring the first 5,000 denarii to Aemilia later tonight. Then, tomorrow morning (Monday) he could start his trip up the mountain, spend the night at the cabin, and then meet Aemilia Tuesday evening with the other 10,000 denarii. But, Nicholas knew he needed a cart or something to bring the money back down the mountain and he didn't have that yet. He was going to have to build or buy a cart to take with him and neither one of those options could happen tonight.

So, they decided that late tomorrow evening, Monday evening, Nicholas would meet Aemilia a couple of roads over – kind of between her house and what was his house just days ago. They figured that it would be best to meet when it was dark so that there would be less risk that someone would see them. At this meeting, Nicholas would give Aemilia the 5,000 denarii he already had. After giving her the money, he would make the incredibly long journey to the cabin and back, nonstop through the night and the next day, to get the rest of the money.

Traveling through the night and roundtrip in one 24-hour period wasn't ideal, but it was the best option they had. So, he would give Aemilia his 5,000 denarii tomorrow on Monday evening, make an overnight roundtrip to his cabin with his yet-to-be-acquired cart, and deliver the other 10,000 denarii on Tuesday evening.

They decided that it would be best not to tell Aemilia's parents. Nicholas and Aemilia weren't comfortable with deceiving them, but they figured it would be best if no one knew where the money was coming from. That way Stephen and Faustina wouldn't have to protect Nicholas, and Alexander wouldn't have any reason to go after Nicholas for more of his money before Nicholas could pay off their entire debt.

With their plan in place, Nicholas walked Aemilia back to her house. At the door they hugged one more time, and Nicholas headed back to Rufus's house for the night.

11 – Monday

Nicholas arrived at Rufus's apartment just before dark that Sunday night. His family was eating dinner when he arrived and Rufus's mom warmly invited Nicholas to join them. After the meal, Nicholas asked Rufus to join him outside so that he could catch up Rufus on everything going on with Aemilia's family and his plan to pay their fine. Rufus wasn't surprised that Nicholas was willing to give up so much money to help Aemilia's family. He was surprised, however, at the immediate change in Nicholas's demeanor from just two days before.

As Nicholas shared his ideas with Rufus, Rufus came up with the idea to build a small cart that Nicholas could use to bring the coins down from the cabin. It took both of their strength to carry the original 5,000 denarii the day before and Nicholas was going to have to go back to the cabin for the rest of the money all by himself. Rufus's dad would not allow Rufus to miss another day of work. He was already angry at Rufus for following Nicholas up the mountain a few days ago, especially without warning him that he would be gone and not working.

So, Rufus decided that he would build the cart after he finished work on Monday and have it ready for Nicholas by Monday evening. Nicholas's plan was to meet Aemilia just after dark on Monday to give her the first 5,000 denarii, then head up to the cabin, towing the cart through the night. He knew that it would take nearly an entire 24-hour day to go to and from the cabin, and he'd have to wait to start his journey until after he gave Aemilia the first 5,000 denarii on Monday evening. He figured he made it up the mountain a few nights ago when he wasn't in good health or in a good mental state, so he should be able to handle it fine now that he was better. After trekking through the night to the cabin, Nicholas would immediately head back down the mountain with all of the money he could carry on the cart. His plan was to be back in town by Tuesday evening, after dark, and meet to give Aemilia the other 10,000 denarii that her family would need to pay off the rest of the debt.

Early Monday morning Nicholas woke up refreshed, but with his head racing. His racing thoughts weren't about his plan to get Aemilia the money, but rather he was ecstatic as he tried to process his feelings toward Aemilia and he was doubly ecstatic as he interpreted that she must be having the same type of feelings toward him. Of course, he was concerned about her family's predicament, but was confident that his plan would work.

Rufus had to be up early to head off to work with his dad, so Nicholas got up early too. He knew he had a long night ahead of him as he would have to stay up all night and all of the next day. Nicholas didn't want to try to sleep during the day at Rufus's apartment – for one, he didn't want Rufus's family to know what he was doing because he was afraid that somehow Alexander would find out, and for two, there would be no possible way to get any rest in Rufus's small apartment with all of Rufus's younger siblings around.

After eating breakfast with Rufus, Nicholas took off to the beach, planning to find a shady area to rest. Rufus's dad said something about how Nicholas should find work and that he wouldn't be able to freeload off them for long. Nicholas wasn't rude, but he declined the offer to join Rufus at work today and promised that he would be able to take care of himself soon.

Nicholas found a secluded spot on the beach and spent the day catnapping, thinking of his possible future with Aemilia and planning what to do with his money after this ordeal was over. Where would he live? What would his occupation be? Did he need an occupation? Of course he needed an occupation – he couldn't be lazy the rest of his life.

Nicholas thought that it was ironic that the first two payments of 5,000 denarii were going to rescue Diantha and Iris. Neither of them would know that it was Nicholas providing the money. He figured that Diantha might even be so stubborn as to refuse the money if she knew it was coming from him. He laughed to himself as he pictured her throwing the coins back at his face, willingly leaving the house as a slave. On the other hand, he figured Iris would try to marry him if she knew he was her savior. "It's best that they never find out," Nicholas thought, laughing to himself.

*** *** *** *** *** *** *** *** *** *** ***

Nicholas woke up out of a deep sleep when his body jerked and he momentarily feared that he slept passed his meeting time with Aemilia. Looking around, he realized that it wasn't quite dark yet, but that the sun was setting. He was thankful that he woke up when he did and his brain quickly started working overtime, thinking about his meeting with Aemilia and his long trip up and down the mountain.

Nicholas nearly forgot that he would need to get the cart before he met Aemilia so that he could waste no time going straight to the cabin after meeting her. He took off in a hurried pace back to Rufus's apartment. He was hopeful that Rufus's cart would do the job. After all, Rufus was always good at building things.

When Nicholas arrived at Rufus's apartment, he first saw Rufus's mother.

"Sit down and eat some dinner," she said to Nicholas as more of an instruction than an invitation.

"No thank you, ma'am. I have a busy evening ahead of me. In fact, I won't be staying here tonight."

Not quite paying attention to Nicholas, Rufus's mom put together a plate of suspicious looking stew and sat it on the table in front of where Nicholas was standing.

Begrudgingly, he thanked her, sat down and tried to eat the bland food quickly so that he could go see Rufus. Nicholas thought to himself, "I should have never come inside to begin with."

Processing that Nicholas said he wouldn't be staying tonight, Rufus's mom seemed a little put off that he was staying somewhere else, silently wondering if Nicholas thought he was too good for their little apartment. She didn't bring it up and Nicholas quickly ate his stew and then found Rufus.

As expected, Rufus had the cart ready for Nicholas.

"Here she is, Nick," Rufus beamed with pride. "It's the best I could do in an hour."

"It looks great Rufus!" Nicholas was truly impressed. The cart was simple, but seemed sturdy. "I can't believe you made this in only one hour."

"I took two old wheels that were left over from something else, attached a few boards, and made a nice, strong handle." Rufus picked up the cart by the handle to show Nicholas how strong it was. "And I tried to make it so that you could work it by yourself."

"Thanks again Rufus. I know that parts of the mountain path aren't going to be the easiest to travel with a cart, but at least it hasn't rained (or snowed) since the storm the other night. So, hopefully the path will be relatively dry."

Nicholas thanked his friend still yet again, gave him a firm hug, and then took his cart and his 5,000 denarii to go meet Aemilia.

Nicholas made this trip across town hundreds of times before. With his dad's barn and Rufus's house so close together, Nicholas made the half-hour trip by himself since he was about eight years old. While he never felt unsafe before, this time was different. He knew he was hauling a lot of money in his cart and lots of dishonest and even temporarily dishonest people would love to have that money. Although he carried the coins to Rufus's apartment yesterday, today he felt less safe. He placed a heavy blanket over the coins and even a few turnips. Rufus had the idea to throw some turnips on top of the blanket with a few underneath, just in case people were curious about what Nicholas was carrying.

As Nicholas went through the center of town, he saw Crispus across the street, the banker who accompanied Alexander to take Nicholas's money days before. Nicholas immediately lowered his head and tried to not make eye contact with him. He wasn't sure if Crispus was a co-conspirator in Alexander's evil plans or just helping Alexander out for a cut of the money.

"He's a banker," Nicholas thought to himself. "He's probably just in it for the money. I bet if I went up to him and offered him 500 denarii to turn on Alexander, he'd do it in a heartbeat."

Of course, Nicholas didn't have any such plans of revenge, though this was the first time that it occurred to him that he would have to deal with Alexander at some time. There would be no doubt that Alexander would be very upset with Stephen and Faustina's debt paid. And, it seemed only a matter of time before Alexander suspected Nicholas.

"I wonder what kind of evil Alexander is capable of?" Nicholas thought.

Nicholas's thoughts turned from wonder to sadness. He felt sad for Crispus – a man so in love with money that he would stoop to any level to make a coin or two. He felt sad for Alexander – a man who didn't have a family and only had so-called friends who simply loved his money and his power.

"What a shame that Alexander's life has become what it is," Nicholas pondered as he continued walking to his meeting point with Aemilia.

A few minutes later it was just getting dark and Nicholas was almost to his rendezvous point with Aemilia. He wondered if she would already be there, worried that he wasn't going to have the money.

Sure enough, Nicholas arrived and Aemilia was already there.

Aemilia was relieved, happy, and a little nervous to see Nicholas. Like Nicholas, she spent most of the day thinking about last evening's kiss and wondering what it all meant to him and for them.

"Hey, Nick," Aemilia spoke playfully and a little flirtatiously when she saw him. "Whatcha' doing out this time of night?"

Aemilia tried to be funny, but when she finished speaking, she held her head slightly down while looking up at Nicholas. She was hoping he would be warm in return and she was hoping to see on his face a return of the feelings she had for him. But, new to these kind of affectionate expressions, she doubted herself and nervously waited for his response.

"Oh, nothing. I'm just out taking these turnips for a ride, looking for someone who will buy them. Would you like any turnips?"

Nicholas was also wondering what Aemilia was thinking. Last evening was so special, but he thought that maybe she had thought about it more throughout the day and come to her senses – angry with him for how he had treated her the last three months.

"I don't know about turnips, but I'm interested in the guy pushing the cart."

Aemilia was horrified! She couldn't believe what came out of her mouth. She wondered if Iris had somehow taken over her tongue and filled it with her silly, flirtatious, embarrassing nonsense.

"Well, the way I see it," Nicholas responded, relieved and inching closer to Aemilia," you can have the turnips and the guy."

Nicholas dropped the handles of the cart and barely got his arms open before Aemilia grabbed him. They hugged each other like they had not seen each other in months. It was as if they were married years ago and Nicholas just got home from fighting in one of Diocletian's wars. For a moment, nothing else mattered. It didn't matter that Aemilia and her sisters were in trouble. It didn't matter that Nicholas had a long, 24-hour journey ahead of him. It didn't matter what Alexander or anyone else thought. For the brief time of that embrace, they were both fully satisfied in life.

"I'm so glad to see you," Nicholas broke the silence and the two loosened their grip, lightly holding each other's arms.

"And I'm glad to see you, Nick."

"I have the money for you – it's 5,000 denarii."

"Where did you get the cart?"

"Rufus made it for me. He whipped it up in about an hour this evening – out of stuff he had lying around the house."

"That Rufus sure is a kind, talented guy."

"Yeah, he's about the best friend a guy could have."

Nicholas reached out and hugged Aemilia again, just as tightly as before.

"As much as I'd like to stay out here all night, you better get home and I better start up the mountain."

"Nick, I just can't believe you are doing that. Really, you don't have to."

"I'm not going to argue about it, Aemilia. It's what I want to do. It's what I have to do."

"Well, thank you. I can't even begin to tell you how much this means to me."

Nicholas looked around to make sure no one was watching and showed Aemilia the two bags of coins totaling 5,000 denarii. They were quite heavy, but she was determined to get them home in one trip. They both thought it would be best if he didn't help her carry them to the house, so they decided that she could do it by herself and he would watch her from a distance. If she had any trouble with people or anything, then Nicholas could spring into action, saving his girl and the money.

Nicholas leaned in for one more hug, but Aemilia moved her head up and gave him a quick kiss on the cheek. Then she grabbed the two bags of coins and, struggling a bit, started walking home. Nicholas thought it was funny that he and Rufus barely got those coins down the mountain between the two of them, and here was Aemilia carrying them all by herself.

He followed her as she walked home – it was just a short two-minute walk. He was careful that he could always see her, but that he also stayed hidden. He peeked around the corner of houses and hid behind bushes. Although the short walk only lasted a few moments, as Nicholas watched Aemilia, she appeared to him in a way he had never seen her before – more beautiful and older than he realized.

Aemilia made it to her front door and turned around, looking for Nicholas. He waved his arm at her, poking half of his body around a nearby house.

Aemilia waved back and threw him a kiss. Nicholas returned a thrown kiss, and turned his cart away from Aemilia's house, starting the journey through town and up the mountain.

To Aemilia's relief, no one was in the living room when she opened the front door. In all of her thinking and planning, she never really considered what to say if someone in her family saw her carrying in the bags of coins.

Seeing no one, she brought in both bags and carefully set them in the living room. Her parents were in their bedroom praying about tomorrow morning. Diantha was in her room arranging her clothes and jars, knowing that she might not see them again. Iris, already accepting that she would soon belong to someone else, was in her room brushing her hair. She figured she might as well look pretty – maybe she'd get the better master out of the three sisters. Aemilia left the money on the floor and quietly went into her room. She knew it could be just a matter of minutes before someone found the bags.

A moment later, Stephen cried out to the rest of the family.

"Everyone! Come here!" Stephen hollered out to his family, excited.

"What is it, daddy?" Diantha asked as she entered the room. It seemed like she was always first.

"What is wrong, dear?" Faustina asked. Her eyes were red from crying.

As Aemilia and Iris entered the room, Stephen was on the floor, dumping out both large bags of coins.

"I just can't believe it! Look at all of this money. Where did it come from?"

"Where did that come from?" Iris asked.

"I don't know," Stephen replied. "Do any of you know?"

"Not me."

"I don't know."

"Not me either."

Everyone else in the family expressed their bewilderment, so Aemilia thought she should chime in as well.

"I don't know, either," Aemilia softly said. She rarely lied to her parents and felt kind of weird about it, but she and Nicholas had agreed that it was best if her family didn't know where the money came from for now.

"Well praise be to God!" Stephen exclaimed. "I don't know where it came from or why it's here, but we need 5,000 denarii by tomorrow morning. Let's see how much is here."

Over the next several minutes the entire family sorted and counted the coins. Diantha kept a record as each person called out their exact amounts.

"5,125 denarii," Diantha confidently exclaimed.

"No fair!" cried Iris. "That's only enough to save Diantha."

"Oh be grateful, Iris," Aemilia snapped back. "One of us is saved, just in time. Who knows about the next day?"

"Aemilia is right," Faustina agreed. "Let's all be grateful that for at least tomorrow we are all going to be OK."

"I think we should sing a song of thanks," Stephen offered. So, the five of them sang a song they learned in church. They spent the rest of the evening grateful and comforted that, for at least one more night, they would all be safe.

12 – Tuesday Morning, Payment 1

Overnight, Nicholas pushed his newly created cart up the mountain. He underestimated how hard it would be to push this seemingly light cart uphill for so many hours. Thankfully the cart stayed together through the entire trip, despite Nicholas's best efforts at damaging it – one time hitting a wheel hard against a tree branch and another time losing control of the cart as it slid down a bank into a shallow creek.

Nicholas was happy the moon was out and nearly full as he made his way up the mountain. Oddly he wasn't tired – he kept focusing on his mission at hand and replaying over and over in his head the scene that must have unfolded at Aemilia's house earlier that evening. He sure hoped that Aemilia would be able to keep their plan a secret. He was genuinely afraid of what might happen if Alexander figured out that Nicholas had more money and that he was using that money to help Aemilia's family.

Nicholas turned his thoughts to Alexander. He wondered what Alexander's reaction would be in the morning when he came to claim Diantha, only to be surprised with the 5,000-denarii payment. Nicholas actually smiled a time or two, imagining Alexander's reaction and disbelief.

Nicholas continued on the long, lonely path up the mountain. Fortunately, the weather was warmer and dryer than a few nights ago. The snow that nearly took his life had melted and the path was generally dry. There were some muddy areas, especially places where the path was more shielded from the new winter's southern sun. It was a good thing that Myra sits on the south side of the mountains because that meant that Nicholas climbed up the southern slope and so there were few places that the sun didn't shine in the winter.

Nicholas arrived at the cabin just after daybreak. He knew he should have made better time, but the weight of the cart really took its toll on Nicholas's pace during the last two hours of the trip. Nicholas didn't have much time – he would have surely loved to take a nap. Stopping his hike at the cabin actually let his body feel just how tired it was. Nicholas looked at the bed that he lay on just a few nights ago, dreaming those weird dreams and eating Rufus's bland soup. He decided he couldn't risk not waking up from a nap, so he began loading the coins.

Nicholas had thought a lot on the hike up the mountain about how much money he should take back with him. Of course, he needed another 10,000 denarii for Aemilia's family, but he also knew that he needed to bring back more money to help him establish the next part of his life. The problem was that he didn't know what would be the next part of his life. For someone whose life suddenly had great purpose and perspective, he ironically didn't know what he was going to do in just two short days.

Nicholas decided to bring 20,000 denarii down the mountain. He figured that the extra 10,000 denarii would be more than enough to help him get on his feet. He was afraid that Alexander might sue him to get more of his money, so he thought it was wise to leave the rest in the cabin.

"After all," he thought, "I might just decide to move up to this cabin and live here!"

Nicholas finished loading the coins and covered them with Rufus's blanket and turnips. The sun was shining brightly now and the crispness of the night gave way to the warmth of the new day. Depending on the weather, the elevation where his cabin sat could be warm in the winter. Thankfully today was one of those days.

"I hope I don't come across too many people," Nicholas thought. He was worried that people would find it suspicious that he was carting a load of turnips down the mountain in December. After all, turnips didn't exactly grow in the mountains in December. He was also afraid that someone might rob him.

Nicholas grabbed a hold of the old handles on the newly made cart and started down the mountain. He had newfound energy in beginning the second leg of his trip. The cart was much heavier than before, but at least he was going downhill.

*** *** *** *** *** *** *** *** *** *** ***

Alexander could hardly sleep as he woke up before daylight on Tuesday morning. As cruel as it seems, he was genuinely excited for today. He had nothing against Diantha. In fact, if he let himself think about it, he might even have felt a little bad that she was going to be sold as a slave. But, all Alexander could think about was how perfectly his plan had gone to go after Stephen. It's funny how Alexander thought he was getting revenge when it was actually Stephen who had shown Alexander mercy by not exposing him years ago. When we get trapped in our own minds, as Alexander often did, we can tend to distort reality in pretty impressive ways.

Alexander left his home at about 8:00 in the morning. He lived close to the center of town and had to stop by the magistrate's office to make his seizure legal. While the law allowed Alexander to sell one child per day until the debt was repaid, it was up to him to contract with the slave trader and any necessary strong men to make sure that everything went as planned.

Alexander went into the magistrate's office and secured the proper paperwork with the magistrate's seal. He had already made arrangements to meet Adrian, a local slave trader, at the magistrate's office. Adrian (usually working with his crafty sister, Kalistrate) was a full-service slave trader, bringing along his own set of men to make sure that everything went OK. Of course, Alexander was paying for the service. Alexander would have to pay Adrian 20 denarii. Normally Alexander would have tried to negotiate a better price, but he was so excited to complete his plan, he was willing to part with the extra money. He didn't even seem to care about the money, which was quite unusual for Alexander.

Alexander paced back and forth outside the magistrate's office as Adrian wasn't there yet.

"Where is that man!" Alexander fumed, looking down each direction of the street with his newly sealed paper in his hand.

"I'll go get her myself if I have to!"

Moments later Adrian and three strong men turned the corner and walked toward Alexander.

"You're late!"

"I'm just on time," Adrian said smoothly, perhaps with more charm and cunning than even Alexander possessed.

"Well, let's get on with it."

Alexander, Adrian, and Adrian's three men walked the fifteen minutes to Stephen and Faustina's home. The same sun that warmed Nicholas in the mountains above and gave him renewed strength for his journey, beat down on Alexander near sea level in Myra.

"Cursed sun!" Alexander scowled. "Phoebus must be hard at work today!" Phoebus was a name Romans used for the god Apollo when he was busy making the sun bright and hot.

In what seemed like an eternity, Alexander and his crew arrived outside of Stephen and Faustina's house.

"Let me do the talking. You stand behind me with one of your men, just so they know we're serious. Have another of your men stand a few feet from the door and the other one behind the house, just in case."

Alexander took a deep breath, walked up to the door, and knocked very loudly and deliberately. He was so excited to see the look on Stephen's face – no doubt a tear-stained face, weary from no sleep and the mourning that comes with losing a child to slavery.

"How sweet it is," Alexander said to Adrian, "Stephen's first child will be plucked from him on this day. All of the hopes, all of the dreams, all of the grandchildren – washed away!"

Alexander tried to remove the smile from his face as the door opened in front of him.

Stephen stepped out through the door and shut it quickly behind him.

"I am here for your oldest daughter, Diantha. I have the paper right here, fresh with a seal from the magistrate's office."

"Well, you can't have her."

"Stephen, let's not let this get ugly. I have every right to take her and I have men here to make sure it happens."

"Well, you can't have her, because I have the money."

"What?!" Alexander was confused, thinking Stephen was bluffing. "You don't understand. The first payment is due right now. Not later. Not tomorrow."

"And I have the first payment right now."

Stephen opened the door, reached into his house, and produced two bags of coins.

"5,000 denarii. Just like required."

"It can't be!" Alexander opened both bags.

"It's all there, count it yourself."

"You, come help," Alexander said to Adrian, motioning for him to come up to the door.

"I'm not here to count money. I'm here to take a slave. Which, by the way, you owe me 20 denarii whether I leave here with a slave or not!"

Alexander was getting red in his face. He started counting the money but was counting so quickly that he lost track of where he was on two separate occasions.

"Trust me, it's all there," Stephen beamed. "But, it's your right to count it all. It probably says so on that paper you've got there."

"20 denarii, Alexander," Adrian called out, actually enjoying the confusion and bewilderment that Alexander was experiencing. Sure, he was helping Alexander, but he always took joy in other people's misery.

Alexander dug through the bags and gave him 20 denarii worth of coins.

"Let's go boys." Adrian called out to his helpers and they started to walk away.

"Hey, wait!" Alexander was still in shock. "The same time on tomorrow morning!"

Adrian nodded and walked away.

Then, Alexander looked at Stephen. "You don't have tomorrow's money, do you?"

"We will have to wait and see," Stephen said, acting confidently on the outside but trying to hide his sudden realization that his celebration today would quickly turn into tears for tomorrow.

Alexander reached up and grabbed the top of Stephen's shirt. "Don't mess with me. Do you have the money or not?"

"I don't have it to give you today. But, we will see if God will provide for tomorrow."

"God! Ha! Remember, no one is allowed to pay it for you – not even your God!" Alexander let go of Stephen's shirt and pointed at him a couple of inches from his face. "Where did you get this money?"

"No one has given me this money – God provided it."

"Oh, that's rubbish! You're speaking like a fool. You might have the money to give me today, but if you don't have the other 10,000 denarii now, then you won't have it tomorrow or the next day. I'll see you tomorrow morning!"

Alexander rushed off, struggling to carry his two bags of coins. Never before had so much money been such a burden on Alexander. He would have much rather been walking off with Diantha than the money.

Stephen went back into his house and the entire family embraced. They cried tears of joy and concern as they celebrated this day's victory and feared the next day.

Diantha was relieved. She knew it was selfish to feel such relief with the fate of her two sisters still undetermined. Her tears were slightly more of joy than of concern, though she would have been embarrassed to say it.

Aemilia was so thankful that today worked out. She worried as Nicholas traveled to and from the cabin. She worried that he might change his mind. She worried that he might be overtaken by thieves. It was not like her to worry so much, but as she embraced her family, she worried.

*** *** *** *** *** *** *** *** *** ***

Alexander went straight to Crispus's bank. He bypassed the normal workers and went into Crispus's office. He talked in one run-on sentence about the events of the morning. He made Crispus count the money, just to make sure it was all there. Crispus finished counting and wrote Alexander a receipt.

Alexander fumed as he walked out the door. His mind swirled.

"How did they get the money?"

"I am certain that there is no one who would trade with Stephen."

"I don't think he had anything to sell – not for that much money. Did he sell something?"

"Certainly he can't get the rest of the money by tomorrow."

"Is there anyone who would break the law and give Stephen that money? Who would do such a thing?"

As he stormed down the street, heading back to his house, Alexander suddenly froze in his tracks. His mind allowed one scenario that he hadn't considered. One scenario that he thought impossible – nearly as impossible as Stephen coming up with the money in the first place.

Thinking slowly and deliberately, Alexander softly said aloud, "Perhaps it is Nicholas."

Alexander didn't have any rational reason to believe that Nicholas could be helping Stephen and Faustina. Of course, he recognized Nicholas's close friendship with Aemilia, but he had no reason to believe that Nicholas had the money to help them. His idea was born more out of paranoia than logic. But, as he slowly started walking again, he became more and more convinced that somehow Nicholas was helping them.

By the time Alexander reached his home, he determined that he would hire a man, perhaps one of Adrian's men, to watch Stephen and his house. Certainly Stephen didn't already have the other 10,000 denarii. After all, Stephen said he didn't have it and surely would have paid it today if he did. So, Alexander would hire a man to make sure that Stephen didn't get the money from anyone – not Nicholas, not anyone.

Shortly after Alexander reached his house, he went back out to Adrian's slave-holding building. He struck up a deal for one of Adrian's men. Alexander instructed the man to go straight to Stephen's house and stay there unless Stephen went somewhere. Alexander ordered the man to follow Stephen wherever he went and report on anyone who came to Stephen's house.

The hired man left Alexander with his mission, went to Stephen's house, and stood across the street from the front door.

*** *** *** *** *** *** *** *** *** *** ***

"That guy's still there, Daddy," Iris said, peering out the window at the strange man who was watching their house like a hawk.

"He's no doubt one of Alexander's men. I think I saw him here this morning when Alexander came with the slave trader." Stephen tugged Iris away from the window, knowing that this might be the last day that he could protect his daughter.

"How's anyone going to help me?" Iris said, crying. "It's not fair. We got enough money for Diantha, but what about me?"

"Perhaps God will provide again. That's all the hope we have," Stephen replied.

Aemilia wasn't a part of their conversation, sitting across the room by herself. As her father and Iris talked, she couldn't help but wonder how she was going to get the rest of the money from Nicholas. They planned to meet again this evening, but she knew the man watching their house would see her leave. Would he follow her? Would he see Nicholas? Would he see her bringing the coins back into the house?

"Perhaps..." she thought, biting her fingernails as she worried, "perhaps I can get just some of the money tonight from Nicholas. Aemilia was thinking about only getting the next payment tonight, 5,000 denarii, instead of all of it at once. She was concerned about trying to sneak 10,000 denarii past the guard, and Aemilia obviously forgot about the 1,500 denarii that her family already had from the contract that her father sold a few weeks ago.

Aemilia thought about it most of the rest of the day. She was worried and kept thinking through scenarios where she would get caught or where Nicholas would get caught. She so wished that she could talk to her parents about it, but she knew that she couldn't risk having them know the plan. It would even be too much of a risk to talk only to her mother, even though she was confident her mother could keep it a secret from her dad. After all, Faustina did manage a purchase or two that Stephen never quite noticed. (At least, he acted like he never noticed.) Regardless, this worry was Aemilia's to bear – perhaps a little more weight than a 17-year-old young woman should have to hold.

13 – Tuesday Night

The early winter's daylight was short lived. Nicholas was just entering town as the sun began to set. He was exhausted, but relieved to be in Myra and relieved to think that the setting sun would mean fewer people on the streets to possibly discover his money.

He had a fairly uneventful trip down the mountain. He lost control of the cart once or twice, but it was never a big deal. One time he did spill a few coins. He picked up what he could, but a few of them fell farther down a bank. He knew he had more than enough money to help Aemilia, so he left them there and continued his trip.

As Nicholas walked past the orphanage, he paused. He was so focused on getting to the cabin that he hardly noticed the orphanage on his way up the mountain last night. Now, with just enough daylight to see it, the orphanage looked different. It wasn't a cheerful place. In fact, it looked very bleak. The laughter he heard from children playing a few days ago masked the terrible condition of the building and the uninviting, barely-inhabitable nature of the structure.

This evening the orphanage was silent – different from the other night. There were no children laughing or playing. The dusk that was setting around him wasn't pierced by lights poking out of the orphanage – there were no lights on that Nicholas could see. Nicholas wondered if Papa Antony might still be there for the day, helping to settle down the children and put them in bed. Perhaps he told them a Bible story. Maybe he scooped up one or two of them, placing them on his lap as he spoke to them.

Nicholas noticed that outside of the orphanage, against the side of the building, were sets of shoes. They were definitely children's shoes and they looked like they had been well-worn. Nicholas wondered about the number of previous owners each pair of shoes must have had. Several pairs had holes in their toes and many had rips on their sides. Nicholas was fascinated by the shoes and walked over to take a closer look.

The first pair was very dirty with freshly caked mud – no doubt a child had a great time in those shoes today or perhaps another day this week. The second pair had holes in both big toes and an extra hole in the little toe of the right shoe.

The third pair was so tiny. "Are there children who are this small in the orphanage?" Nicholas thought. Of course, there were. Nicholas realized that poverty and ill fortune were not prejudiced based on age.

After the third pair of shoes were about a dozen other pairs – different sizes, but all dirty and all worn.

Nicholas reached into his bag and decided to leave a coin in each pair of shoes. He wasn't sure what would become of it – maybe the children would keep it a secret and hide them. Maybe they would give the money to Papa Antony who could use it to buy food or even more shoes.

Nicholas started to randomly select coins out of his bag, deciding it was fun to not know what he was placing in each shoe. About seven pairs of shoes into his generous gift-giving, Nicholas had a thought that perhaps distributing the coins unevenly would cause problems with the children. So, he collected his previously-distributed coins and dug through his bag to find enough of the same coin for each pair of shoes.

Nicholas placed the coins in the shoes, then went back to the third pair of shoes – the smallest pair – and placed an extra coin in the tiny pair of shoes. "This little person deserves a little extra joy," Nicholas thought.

Nicholas continued through town and over to Aemilia's neighborhood. By now it was dark – the clouds covered the moonlight and the only light in town was from torches and candles lit on the opulent houses around Aemilia's house.

Nicholas went to the same spot where he met Aemilia the night before. A little bit ago he really felt the effects of his 24-hour trip, just before he got to Myra's edge. Now, however, he was refreshed and excited to see Aemilia. He was excited to hear about how the morning went and about how Alexander reacted. He was most excited to give Aemilia the rest of the money so that her father could pay off both debts tomorrow morning – for Iris and for her. Then, this entire ordeal would be over.

Nicholas waited and waited, wondering what was taking Aemilia so long. He kept looking for her as the evening wore on later and later. He was starting to get worried. "What if something happened?" he thought. "What if Alexander figured out that I gave them the money and then he took them all away?"

Just when Nicholas's head was racing with increasingly insurmountable scenarios, Aemilia came walking around the corner, looking behind her and wearing fear on her face.

At first Nicholas smiled when he saw her, but then he realized that she was scared.

"What's the matter Aemilia? Is everything OK? Did it go as planned this morning?"

"Yes, it went very well, actually. But now Alexander is so mad that he has hired a guard to watch our house. He's been out there all day. I barely snuck out of the side window. I was so afraid he'd see me."

"I'm so sorry Aemilia. How did you do it?"

"I watched him all afternoon. He hardly ever left his spot across from our house. The only thing that kept him from watching our house was when my neighbor three doors down came out of her house to throw something out or clean something. I guess it's a good thing that Nestor married someone so pretty." Aemilia chuckled, referring to her neighbor Nestor and his beautiful wife, Helene.

"Anyway, the closer it got to when I needed to leave, I stayed by my bedroom window on the side of the house. I could still barely see him watching the house. Just a few minutes ago, Helene came out of her house, the guard couldn't keep his eyes off her, and I went as quickly and as quietly as possible through my bedroom window and out toward the back of house."

"Are you sure he didn't see you? Did he follow you here?"

"No, I'm certain he didn't."

"OK, then. Try and relax. Everything will be OK."

Without hesitating or overthinking if he should, Nicholas reached out and held Aemilia, squeezing her tightly and comforting her.

Aemilia, usually one to not focus on herself, suddenly remembered that Nicholas had been up and down the mountain in the last 24 hours.

Aemilia released her equally tight grip on Nicholas and asked, "How did your trip go? You must be so tired."

"It went well. I'm a little tired, but I feel good right now. I figure I must be on my eighth wind or something."

"Were you able to get the money? I almost feel ashamed asking. How did Rufus's cart do?"

"His cart did splendidly! He is really talented. Yes, I was able to get the money – plenty enough for you and plenty for me to figure out what I'm doing next."

Aemilia, feeling secure for the first time since she saw the guard outside her house earlier in the day, reached over and hugged Nicholas.

Without thinking, she blurted, "Nick. I owe you so much. I think I love you."

Nicholas was a little taken aback and probably hesitated a little too long. Aemilia shrunk back a bit, then Nicholas gathered his thoughts and said, "Aemilia, I've been giving it a lot of thought. After all, someone made me stay up for the last 24 hours straight, so I've had plenty of time to think!" Nicholas, chuckling, was trying to break the tension. Aemilia pushed him away in playful anger, but then returned to his outstretched arms.

"Anyway, I've been thinking about it a lot. And, well, Aemilia, I do love you too. I really do. I really…"

Before he could emphasize his love with another repeated statement, Aemilia reached up and kissed Nicholas. This kiss was much better than their first kiss – a full testament of their newly declared love for each other.

They pulled slightly away and looking into each other's eyes, Aemilia remembered her predicament.

"Nick, we have a problem. That guard is watching like a hawk. There's no way I can sneak 10,000 denarii into the house. I'm pretty sure I can't even carry it in one trip, and I'm too nervous to try and get away with two trips tonight."

"Maybe I can carry a bag for you."

"There's no way. You'll be thrown into jail and then the money won't count for Iris and me. I was thinking that maybe tonight I should only get enough coins to get through tomorrow morning. Then after that we can figure out a way to get the last payment."

"Aemilia, I really want to get this all over with."

"Me too, but it's just too risky. I just know that I can't carry 10,000 denarii – I barely got 5,000 home last night. This is the best plan, perhaps the only plan – if I can even sneak it past the guard tonight. I'm pretty worried, actually."

Nicholas and Aemilia forgot about their newly declared love and allowed the burden of the situation to weigh on their minds. For perhaps the first time since he found out about the possible slavery situation, Nicholas remembered that Aemilia could very well be sold into slavery in two days. And, if their plan failed – if the guard found Aemilia with the money or if Alexander found out Nicholas was providing the money – then

Aemilia could be sold into slavery as soon as tomorrow morning. Nicholas had even considered that he could simply purchase Aemilia out of slavery, but he knew that the slave traders could hold onto Aemilia for a long, terrible time before selling her. And, he was afraid that somehow Alexander might not allow it.

"OK, then you should just take enough for tomorrow. How much do you have left from this morning?"

"Not very much at all." Aemilia was so focused on Nicholas's help that she forgot her family had 1,500 denarii from their one previously sold contract.

"All right, then you should take 5,000 denarii." He paused. "Then we can do this same thing tomorrow night for the last payment. How about you take 5,000 tonight and 5,000 tomorrow night – nice and even?"

"OK, that sounds like a good plan, Nick. I better get back before someone discovers I'm gone. I'm just not sure how I'm going to get past him."

"How about I'll follow you. When you get near your house, I'll call out to the guard from the other direction. Don't worry, I'll make sure he doesn't see me. Then you can hurry along the wall to the window that you came out of."

With the plan in place, Nicholas and Aemilia hugged one last time. They both started walking to her house. When they got to the set of houses across the road, Nicholas went around to the other side to distract the guard's gaze away from Aemilia's entrance.

When he arrived, he and Aemilia looked at each other. Nicholas nodded and called out, "Hey, who is that? What's going on?"

The guard, just for a moment, turned to look toward where Nicholas was calling out and took three steps toward him. Then, realizing that his job was to stay at Stephen's house, he stopped and turned back around. The three steps were just enough time for Aemilia to emerge from the shadows, moving as quickly as she could with the bag of coins. She was trying so carefully to not make any noise – she especially didn't want the money to clank as she moved it.

With both hands wrapped around the money and trying to muffle any sound it might make, Aemilia made it to the darkness against the side of her house just before the guard turned around to return to his post. With more strength than she thought she possessed and a slight grunt that was louder than she intended, Aemilia heaved the money bag through the window. She froze for a moment, looking at the guard who had returned to carving a stick with his knife. Then she lifted herself up and also went through the window.

Aemilia successfully carried the money into the living room, where for the second night in a row she was able to place the money in the middle of the floor undetected. Aemilia retreated to her bedroom and had just lain down on her bed when her mother cried out.

"Everyone! Come to the living room! It happened again!" Faustina couldn't believe her eyes.

"What?... How?... Where?..." Stephen couldn't even put together two words to make a sentence as he walked into the living room and tried to process what was going on.

With everyone else beating her to the living room, Iris slowly walked in with red, puffy eyes, resigned to tomorrow morning's fate.

"What is it? Is it money for me?" Iris asked.

"Yes, dear," Stephen replied, "it appears to be the money needed for you."

And, for the second night in a row, the family rejoiced together and cried together – confident that they had been given one more day and that they were now two-thirds of the way to overcoming this ordeal. Everyone else except Aemilia slept solidly that night, confident that whoever or however they were getting this money would surely continue into the third day as well. Aemilia, however, slept very little that night, alternating between recalling Nicholas's declaration of love and the true horror that she still might be sold into slavery.

Nicholas took his cart of coins and made it across town on the fuel of excitement from his love for Aemilia. He reached Rufus's apartment where his friend let him in and Nicholas fell promptly asleep.

14 – Wednesday Morning, Payment 2

Wednesday morning started much like the previous morning. Alexander went to the magistrate's office to get the paper and the seal. He met Adrian outside, who was late again. And, together, with Adrian's two other men, they marched to Stephen and Faustina's house.

Alexander was certain Stephen didn't have the money this time. When they arrived, they found the third man, the one who Alexander hired to watch over the house, still at his post, miraculously awake.

"Well, did anything happen?" Alexander asked eagerly.

"No sir. No one went in and no one went out."

"And you're sure of it?"

"Absolutely sure, sir."

Alexander grinned from ear to ear. "Excellent! There's no way Stephen has the money today. Adrian, let's go get a slave!"

Alexander walked up to the house with Adrian a few steps behind him.

Yesterday's knock was bold and deliberate, but today's knock seemed to be that again with a touch of arrogance. Alexander, proud of his loud knock, stepped back and waited for the door to move.

The door opened, just wide enough for Stephen to step out.

"OK, Stephen. Today's the day. You can't possibly have the money and I have the paperwork. Bring me your second daughter!"

"Alexander, I have always thought of you to be a decent man. Really! I mean, deep down, I believe that you are good and want to do what is right."

"Save it Stephen! I am in the right in demanding your daughter. You owe me and you cannot pay. I am right and there's nothing you can do about it."

"Well my old friend, there is something." And after saying that, Stephen cracked open the door and produced the bag of coins. "Here it is, 5,000 denarii."

Alexander looked down at the freshly produced bag of coins, then slowly turned up to Stephen, and then slowly back down again to the coins. At first speechless, he cried out, "Impossible! Who is helping you?! No one is allowed to help you!"

Alexander burst into the house, with Adrian and his men following him.

"Search the house! Someone must be here! Look for money!"

Stephen could do nothing to stop the men as they barged into the house and tore through their belongings. Faustina and the girls hunched in the corner, Iris screaming and Diantha yelling at them to leave. In a matter of seconds, the five men went through the entire house, meeting back in the living room.

"I didn't find anyone."

"Me either!"

"Nope, not me either."

As Alexander received the hasty reports, Adrian walked into the living room with two bags of coins. It was the 1,500 denarii that Stephen and Faustina had from selling the only contract he could sell over the last two weeks and the little bit left over from their first two payments to Alexander.

"What is this?" Alexander asked. "Where are you getting your money?"

"That is honest money, money I made from sales. And, besides, it's all I have."

Alexander looked at Stephen and looked in the coin bags.

Adrian, who had been quickly estimating their contents, said, "There's probably only one or two thousand denarii in here."

"Just over 1,500, to be more exact," Stephen replied. "Unfortunately, not enough to pay tomorrow's payment. But, God will provide."

"God will provide! God will provide!" Alexander mocked Stephen in a whiny, childish voice. "God will provide you nothing!" Turning to the other men, he said, "Are you sure there's no other money?"

The other four men agreed that this money was all that there was in the house.

Alexander, still mad, fumed, "Well, Stephen, it looks like your second-born daughter is safe today. But, mark my words, tomorrow I am coming for your youngest! And there's nothing you can do about it! I'll make sure that no one helps you – not your God or Zeus or anyone!" Looking at Aemilia, Alexander sneered, "I'll see you tomorrow, my love!"

Alexander stormed out the door. He barked at Adrian, "Have your men watch this house. I don't care what it costs! And go find more men! No one gets in and no one gets out of this house!"

Adrian, not too happy to take orders, but more than happy to charge Alexander double for the use of his men, complied. He promised to bring a dozen more men in the next hour.

*** *** *** *** *** *** *** *** *** *** ***

Nicholas woke up late that morning to Rufus's little twin brother and sister poking his feet and laughing. He felt rested from his long sleep – much overdo from his 24-hour hike up and down the mountain.

Nicholas laughed and waved the children off. He lay there, thinking about how well last night went. He just imagined the sight on Alexander's face when he found out Aemilia's family had today's 5,000 denarii.

"Just one more," he thought. "One more payment and it is all over."

Despite the comfort of lying in bed, Nicholas made himself get up and begin his day. He greeted Rufus's mother, who told him that Rufus was at work with his father. She also said something about Rufus's father wondering how long he was staying and Nicholas assured her that it would only be another night or two.

Nicholas decided that he wanted to spend part of the day with Papa Antony. Nicholas had been especially moved by the children in the orphanage and he suspected that maybe God was calling him to do something more than be a secret coin provider. After his visit at the orphanage, Nicholas planned to go to his parents' taken house. He wasn't sure if he could get in or if he was even allowed to go in, but he wanted to look around and grab a few things.

As Nicholas began his walk, he was struck by the warmth of the sun, the brightness of the grass, and the songs of the birds. Everything seemed more alive to him.

Nicholas walked through the main part of town, thinking about last night, about his soon-to-be visit with Papa Antony, about tonight's third payment, and about his future with Aemilia.

When he reached the town's center, he heard the town crier yell out, "Hear ye, hear ye! Let it be known to the citizens of Myra that a large contingent of the army of Gaius Aurelius Valerius Diocletianus, emperor of the Roman Empire, will be arriving in town today or tomorrow. Fear not! They come for quick business and will sail on soon after they arrive."

As the crier spoke, people on the street began excitedly talking of the army's arrival. It was a big deal for such a city as Myra to be noticed by the emperor, even if it was just his army.

Nicholas wasn't looking where he was going, watching the crier and listening to the public's reaction, when he happened to run into and knock over Alexander, who was also walking through town at the same time.

"Watch where you're going, you fool!" Alexander sneered, picking himself up from the ground and not noticing who he was talking to.

"Oh, Alexander. Excuse me. I wasn't paying attention to where I was walking." Nicholas was surprised and overcome with fear when he realized he ran into Alexander.

Alexander looked at Nicholas and, realizing who he was, gave him a long stare before finally speaking.

"Well, if it isn't Nicholas." Alexander started speaking in a harsh tone, then quickly softened as he realized his opportunity to find out if Nicholas had any part in Aemilia's family's unexpected money. Instead of being rude, Alexander turned on his naturally fake charm.

"Nicholas, my dear boy. How are you doing?" He paused only long enough to take a breath. "Oh, actually, before you answer, let me tell you about your house. I didn't want to take it, you see. I owed the banker so much money and your payment was short.... It was the magistrate's decision, actually. I didn't want it, but it is the law."

"Yes, Alexander, it seems I've been learning a lot about the law lately."

With that comment, Nicholas and Alexander just awkwardly looked at each other, each knowing that Nicholas was referring to Alexander's treatment of Aemilia's family. Alexander, deciding to press Nicholas a little bit, partly relaxed his fake charm and spoke.

"Well, Nicholas, the law is the law. There's nothing we can do about that. Just be good Romans and all." Alexander paused.

"Tell me, Nicholas, what was the name of that nice young girl at your funeral…? Uhm, I think Stephen and Faustina's daughter?"

"I think you know her name, Alexander. Or do you not care to learn the names of the lives you are ruining?"

With that comment, Alexander completely let go of his charm and was ensued with rage. "Listen here, son. The LAW is the LAW and you can't do anything about it! If I find out that you are having anything to do with helping Stephen and Faustina, then I'll have you, them and that pretty girl all arrested and sold into slavery! You are nothing! You own nothing of your father's business. It's all mine. Even your house! All mine!"

Nicholas, enjoying Alexander losing his cool, pressed him a little bit. "What's wrong Alexander? You act like things aren't going according to plan!"

Alexander grabbed Nicholas's shirt and pulled Nicholas toward him. Nicholas wasn't scared – there were plenty of people looking at them by now.

"You stay out of this you weak, young boy. You're weak, just like your father, and look where it got him!"

Nicholas wanted to react to the statement about his father, but he took a deep breath and shook Alexander's hand off his shirt.

Alexander continued, "If I catch you anywhere near that girl's house, then I'll personally see to it that you spend the rest of your life in prison or as a slave."

Nicholas maintained his composure and looked Alexander in the eyes. He didn't want to be snide like Alexander, but he couldn't help himself being just a little snarky. He spoke softly and slowly, "Well Alexander, God will provide."

Alexander stormed off, yelling back at Nicholas, "Stay away from her! I'm watching you!"

With Alexander walking off, Nicholas had mixed emotions. On the one hand, he was overrun with a sense of calm about this first encounter with Alexander after everything that happened with his money, his house, and his new perspective on life. On the other hand, he started to think more about the money he still needed to get to Aemilia, wondering how he would get it to her and how Alexander would probably try to keep it from happening.

He was thinking about this as he continued walking to the orphanage. When he arrived, he temporarily forgot about this evening's dilemma and was excited to see Papa Antony outside playing with the children.

"Papa Antony, how are you doing?"

"Nicholas, what a pleasant surprise!" Papa Antony motioned for the children to come near him and he introduced Nicholas.

"Children, this is Nicholas. Nicholas is a good friend of mine. He attends church with me."

In a dissonance that somehow sounded sweet to Nicholas's ear, each child simultaneously greeted Nicholas with a "hello" or "hi" or some other greeting.

"Hello," Nicholas said back. "Is Papa Antony treating you well?"

"Yes," one blond-headed boy spoke up, probably about seven years old. "He treats us very well... and God does too!" The boy reached into his pocket and pulled out a shiny coin.

"Oh my," Nicholas said, "that is a nice coin."

"I have one too!"

"Me too!"

"Me too!"

"It seems," Papa Antony explained, "that God used someone to bless these children with a coin in each of their shoes last night. It's truly remarkable!"

"That's really neat," Nicholas said, warmed by the smiles that his simple act inspired.

"Well, you didn't come here to see some coins. What brings you here Nicholas?" As he spoke, he motioned to the children to go into the orphanage. He put his arm around Nicholas and walked him inside.

The inside of the orphanage didn't look anything like Nicholas's dream. There was no long hall with many doors. In fact, it was basically one large room with bunk beds on one side, a table on the other, and some meager toys strung about on the floor. It would have been a completely sad scene if not for the laughing and playing children.

"Papa Antony," Nicholas said, getting down to business, "I really believe that God is calling me to something – something bigger than I am."

"It would seem that way, Nicholas."

"You talked about tugs in your heart, people saying things, dissatisfaction. I think I have all of those things, too."

"Well, Nicholas, perhaps God is calling you to be a priest." Papa Antony looked deeply into Nicholas's eyes. Nicholas almost felt like Papa Antony must be able to see straight into his heart.

Papa Antony looked toward the children and waved his arm. "This is what it is about, Nicholas. Serving these little ones. Serving the church. Serving other people. I have great joy in my life from these things, but they do come with a cost."

"What kind of cost?"

"This isn't a way to become rich, and that might be difficult for you because you knew what it was to be rich. And, this job comes with the weight of so many people – their worries and fears, their difficulties, even their salvation."

"I think I can handle that, Papa Antony. No, I believe I can handle it. I want to handle it."

"Well, Nicholas, it seems that you very well could. Give God a little more time – you've just experienced great changes in your life. If God wants you as a priest, then he won't let you go so easily. And, who knows, perhaps God will use your life to impact little ones like these."

Just then the little blond-headed boy threw a ball of yarn toward Nicholas. Nicholas threw it back, which invited all of the children to begin playing with, and ultimately wrestling with, Nicholas.

Nicholas fell to the floor and Papa Antony let out one of his deep-bellied laughs. Nicholas was laughing too when his necklace came out from under his shirt.

The children were mesmerized – it was such a bright, shiny gold necklace.

"Wow! That must be worth a million aurei!" one child exclaimed!

"That looks like something Diocletian would own!" another child said.

Nicholas laughed. "Ha. I doubt Diocletian would own this. This necklace is a sign of my faith, passed down from my great-grandfather to my grandfather, who passed it down to my father and then to me."

The children oohed and ahed at the necklace.

Papa Antony took a special interest in it. "Let me take a look at it, Nicholas."

Papa Antony inspected the necklace and its design.

Nicholas explained, "My great-grandfather made it to remind himself of his faith. The story goes that he wanted to be able to remind himself of his faith without other people necessarily knowing what it meant, just in case he got in trouble for it or something.

"He made the necklace to represent the Trinity – three different parts of the necklace to represent each part of the Trinity. Instead of a straight cross, he chose the Greek letters chi and rho layered on top of each other to represent Jesus." (The Greek letter "chi" looks like the letter "x," and "rho" looks like a "p.")

"He figured that not only do they spell the first two letters of "Christ," but when placed on top of each other, also kind of look like a cross. I personally think he was using a little artistic freedom!" Nicholas laughed and Papa Antony laughed in kind.

"What about the rest of the necklace?" Papa Antony asked.

"The circle around the chi rho symbol represents God the Father. It is supposed to represent his eternal power and knowledge. You know, eternity – like how a circle never ends."

"Very nice. And the curvy lines?"

"He used the three wavy lines to represent the Holy Spirit. He figured that was a good way to represent something so abstract."

"I see. Well, that is a very nice necklace and a very nice reminder of your faith. Make sure to always wear it and be reminded of both your faith and your parents."

"I will."

Nicholas played with the children for another few minutes and told Papa Antony that he would be coming around a lot more in the future. Nicholas said his goodbyes, slipped a few coins into Papa Antony's coat pocket, left the orphanage, and continued walking on toward his former house.

Nicholas was deep in thought as he walked to his house. As the walk wore on, Nicholas began worrying more about getting Aemilia the 5,000 denarii later this evening and about his encounter with Alexander earlier this afternoon. Alexander said that he'd be watching Nicholas and Nicholas figured that he might be telling the truth. Just before getting to his house, he took a detour and decided instead that he had to see what Aemilia's house looked like – were there guards actually outside her house?

He took an odd route to Aemilia's house, careful not to be seen by too many people. Sure enough, as he peeked around the corner and saw her front door, there were three men at the door and a couple of men across the street. Nicholas walked around the block to get a view of the back of Aemilia's house and saw two more men there. One side of Aemilia's house touched her neighbor's house and the other side had two more men standing in the small alley between Aemilia's house and the house on that side (Alexia's house – the neighbor who Nicholas talked to on Sunday when Aemilia wasn't home).

"This is going to be nearly impossible," thought Nicholas. His worry about how to get tonight's money to Amelia deprioritized visiting his old house. He determined that going into his old house would have to wait until another day. He really needed to get back to Rufus and talk to him about his problem. Certainly, his friend could help him come up with a plan – it was clear that Aemilia wasn't going to be able to meet him this evening, at least not without an escort of guards following her. So, at about 4:00 in the afternoon, Nicholas walked the 30-minute walk across town to Rufus's house. He hoped that Rufus would not be working late today. Nicholas really needed Rufus's help to come up with a good plan for tonight.

15 – The Plan

Nicholas was relieved when he arrived at Rufus's house and Rufus was already home.

"Hey, Nick, did you get caught up on your sleep?"

"Yes!" Nicholas said emphatically. "I really needed it and it was good to get!"

"Awesome! So, are you relieved it's all over?"

Nicholas realized that he fell right asleep last night and never got to tell Rufus about how Aemilia had to sneak out of and back into her house, in addition to his encounter with Alexander earlier today and all of the guards at Aemilia's house that evening. So, he filled in his friend of those events and shared with him his dilemma for this evening.

"I just don't know how I'm going to do it, Rufus. How am I going to get Aemilia the last 5,000 denarii? I've got to do it. She's on the line now. It's not Diantha or Iris – it's Aemilia. I think I love her."

Nicholas didn't usually share much of his emotions with Rufus (or anyone for that matter) and couldn't believe it came out of his mouth.

"Whoa there, boy! Slow down." Rufus was a little surprised by Nicholas's bold proclamation, but he took it in stride. "So, we need a plan."

Nicholas looked at Rufus, ready for him to come up with an amazing idea. They both paused, Rufus staring at the ceiling and Nicholas staring at Rufus.

Rufus spoke and Nicholas got excited. "How many guards did you say?"

Nicholas was disappointed that Rufus wasn't sharing a grand plan. "I don't know. I could see at least nine."

The boys sat in silence again. Rufus was deep in thought and Nicholas looked at him, waiting for his friend to come through.

"And how much money?" Rufus spoke again, at first exciting Nicholas and then causing him to be a little impatient.

"I told you! 5,000 denarii."

Still more silence. Now Nicholas stared off to the side, trying to come up with an idea, but more or less sitting in despair.

"OK, I have an idea."

Nicholas looked at Rufus and sat on the edge of his seat.

"It's clear that Aemilia can't come to you and it is clear that you can't take the coins to her."

"Yes, I am clear on that. Do have any ideas on things that I'm not clear on?"

"So, we need a way to get the coins to her – another way."

"Yes, that's the idea." Nicholas was losing hope that his friend could help him. He sat back in his chair and slumped his shoulders.

"So, I've got it!"

Nicholas moved to the edge of his seat again.

"All of the houses in Aemilia's neighborhood are close together. Many of them touch each other."

"Yes, go on."

"So, how about you take the money and get to her house on the roof? You can start several houses over – far enough away, I think, that the guards won't see you. And then you can sneak from roof to roof until you get to her house."

"OK, OK." Nicholas thought for a second. "I think I like this idea."

Nicholas thought some more and added to Rufus's plan. "Then I can let the money down into her house – through a window maybe."

"No, that's too risky – people will see you reaching over the edge of the roof." Rufus said, prompting more silence.

"I'll cut a hole in her roof if I have to!"

A little out of character, Rufus rolled his eyes and shot Nicholas a condescending look. Then Rufus asked, "How about her chimney? They have a chimney, if I remember correctly. You could let the money down through the chimney!" (Even during most of the winter, fireplaces were used primarily for cooking, not for heat. Therefore, there wouldn't likely be a fire in the fireplace at night.)

"That's a great idea Rufus! They do have a chimney."

"Now, you'll have to do it when it's dark enough, but with the moon, they still might see you. Your clothes are pretty bright and I think you're going to need a disguise."

More silence.

"I've got an idea!" Nicholas was excited to come up with something on his own for the plan. "I can get my dad's dirty old coat. It's in my house – I'll just sneak in and get it. It's far from bright and I don't think anyone would recognize me in it."

"That's a great idea, Nicholas. I'll come with you tonight and help you however I can. I can watch from across the street and warn you if necessary."

"Thanks Rufus, you're a good friend. And I knew you'd come up with a good plan."

"No problem, Nick. I even have some sailing rope lying around here somewhere. You can use that to drop the money down the chimney."

The young men chatted a little more about their plan and ate some food. Rufus's mom wasn't sure why they couldn't stay for dinner – she was starting to get a little annoyed at her new houseguest's odd habits. Rufus kissed his mom on the cheek and they left with the bag of coins and Rufus's rope to go get the old coat from Nicholas's former house.

About the same time that Nicholas and Rufus left Rufus's house, Alexander stopped by Aemilia's house to check on how things were going.

"Anything going on here, Adrian? Anything at all?" Adrian was at the house because Alexander was paying him to personally supervise the guards.

"Nope, boss. Nobody has gone in and nobody has come out." Adrian didn't really view Alexander as his boss, but Alexander was paying him good money and Adrian had Alexander's knack for making people feel important.

"Well, let's keep it that way. I don't want there to be any way that Stephen gets any more money."

"How do you think he got the money the first two times? Did he have some saved up or sell something?"

"I don't know!" Alexander gruffed. "I know he didn't have the money to begin with or he would have paid the fine in the first place. I traveled all over Myra and beyond and sent word to everyone I could think of to make sure that no one, and I mean no one, gave Stephen money or bought anything of his.

"I know he sold one of his pottery contracts to a guy from Patara who happened to be in town. He only made 1,500 denarii off of it and I didn't find out about it until about an hour after it happened. So, that explains most of the money we found in his house this morning. I don't know where he is getting the rest of the money. All I can guess is that someone is giving him money secretly every night."

"Someone is *illegally* giving him money," Adrian reminded him, emphasizing the word illegally, which isn't a word that usually bothered Adrian. He didn't often find himself on the right side of the law.

"Yes, someone is *illegally* giving him money," Alexander emphasized the same word as Adrian, but with a patronizing accent.

Although he recognized the patronization, Adrian decided he needed to let Alexander be the boss for today, so he let it slide.

"So, who do you think is giving them the money?"

"My only decent guess is Nicholas – you know, Epiphanius's son. But I know for a fact that I took…" Alexander cleared his throat and corrected himself, "that I *received* all of his money in our perfectly legal business exchange. Unless he had money stashed somewhere, and I don't see how he could have, then I don't understand how he could be the one providing the money."

Alexander continued, "On the other hand, I know that he has a thing for that youngest girl, Aemilia. So, if he had a way, then he certainly had the motivation to help them. That won't happen a third time though!"

"You're right about that!"

Alexander and Adrian stood in silence for a minute or two. Adrian acted like he was busy surveying the perimeter and monitoring his men and Alexander began to think more and more about Nicholas.

Breaking the silence, Alexander spoke. "I could have taken him in, you know. I could have taken in Nicholas after his parents died."

He paused for a moment. This was an odd turn in the conversation that made Adrian a little uncomfortable – Adrian wasn't too much into feelings and compassion.

"Maybe I should have, but it would have been way too much work – training him in the business. His father didn't do a great job training him, and besides, I would have had to retrain him to do things the way I like them, if you know what I mean!" Alexander looked at Adrian and winked – both men laughed.

"Regardless," Alexander lost his brief compassionate demeanor, "if Nicholas is the one providing the money, then I'll have him thrown into jail."

Again, there was silence. During this silence Alexander thought more about how Nicholas was acting just like Epiphanius and how that Alexander never liked Epiphanius's care for other people. He always thought that he and Epiphanius could have made more money and amassed more power if Epiphanius would have embraced doing business a little more dishonestly. It actually started to make Alexander angry.

"I'll do more than throw him in jail. I'll throw him in jail, and then I'll buy that pretty girl of his and make her my own slave. That will teach him."

Alexander's anger fueled itself.

"He thinks he is so good." Then Alexander spoke with a mocking voice, "Look at me, I'm a good Christian. I'm helping people."

Using his regular voice again, Alexander said, "He's just a law breaker – he's not some Christian saint."

Then, mocking again, he said, "The Saint of Myra. That's what he thinks he is – Saint Nicholas of Myra." Alexander walked around and waved like a princess. Pretending to pass out coins to his subjects, he proclaimed, "I am Saint Nicholas and here, you can have some money. And you can have some money." Turning to Adrian, Alexander mocked, "And you – God loves you. And, oh yeah, your sins are forgiven."

Adrian wasn't sure how to respond, so he just stayed quiet. Alexander seemed pretty obsessed with the idea that Nicholas was providing Stephen the money. Adrian wasn't so sure, but he didn't have his own explanation. He was sure, however, that tonight no one would be getting in or out of that house.

Inside the house, Stephen, Faustina, Diantha, Iris, and Aemilia spent time praying, then crying, then praying, then crying. While the rest of the family didn't know how the money appeared the first two nights, Aemilia knew that Nicholas provided it and she also knew that there was no way she could leave the house this evening to get the last 5,000 denarii.

Aemilia often walked to the window, looking out at the guards, hoping that they would just give up and go home. She trusted Nicholas and she trusted God – she just really hoped that both would pull through for her tonight.

*** *** *** *** *** *** *** *** *** *** ***

Nicholas and Rufus arrived at Nicholas's former house to get the old coat about an hour before sunset. They paused outside the house for a few minutes, and looking around to make sure that no one was watching, they tried to determine if anyone was inside.

Instead of walking up to the front door, they snuck around all four sides of the house, peeking in the windows and quietly listening, to be certain that no one was there.

As confident as they could be that no one was in the house, they walked up to the front and entered through the unlocked door.

"Interesting," Nicholas whispered. "The notice says it is Alexander's house, but it doesn't look like anyone has been here the last few days."

"I suppose Alexander only has so much time in the day to ruin people's lives. I'm sure he plans to get to your house after he ruins Aemilia's life. His list of evil plans is pretty long – there's only so much time in one day," Rufus whispered back, trying to funny.

Nicholas dropped the bag of coins and rope inside the front door and walked around the rooms of the house with Rufus more or less following behind him. Although it was his house just a few days ago, the house felt foreign to him – like it was full of things that didn't really matter anymore. He spent a few extra minutes in his parents' bedroom. That was something he rarely did in the entire three months since they died in the fire. He looked at jewelry, clothing, and other things, trying to recall memories that each object inspired.

After a little bit of time in the house, Rufus spoke up, this time not whispering. "Nick, we better get going. It's going to get dark soon."

"You're right Rufus, we need to get to Aemilia's house to check everything out. I think the best way onto the roofs of the connecting houses is Sebastian's house, five houses down from Aemilia's house. But I guess that's something we need to figure out before it gets too dark."

The boys started to walk out the front door when Nicholas remembered the reason they went to the house in the first place – the dirty, brownish-red coat.

"Oh yeah, the old coat!" Nicholas exclaimed.

"I can't believe we almost left without it, Nick."

Nicholas went back into his bedroom where he had thrown the dirty coat into the corner the night that he brought it back from the barn. He picked it up off the floor, shook it out, and held it up to inspect it.

"I think this will work well. It covers most of my body and it is so dirty that the red has faded and won't draw any attention to it."

Nicholas draped the coat over his arm, grabbed the bag of coins and rope by the door, and left his former house with his friend. Nicholas realized that Rufus was probably right – Alexander would likely turn his attention to this house soon. Nicholas decided that he would have to come back to the house in the next day or two to try and get more of his things out of the house before Alexander moved in.

They walked the short walk to Aemilia's house and took up the same position Nicholas had used earlier in the day when he first saw the guards. Rufus, seeing the guards for the first time, finally realized what a dangerous task his friend was about to undertake.

16 – Wednesday Night

Alexander was still with Adrian when Nicholas and Rufus arrived, although with the cloud cover it was just barely too dark for the boys to recognize that he was there. Aemilia and her family had just finished their time of praying and crying.

Now getting late, Aemilia's parents kissed each of their daughters and gave Aemilia an especially long hug.

"God will work it out," Faustina said. "He has the other two times and he will do it again this time."

Even though the family spent time praying and crying, everyone except Aemilia had a much stronger dose of confidence this third night than what they had experienced the first two nights. In their own ways and to varying degrees, they figured that since it all worked out the first two nights, then it would surely work out this night as well.

Aemilia felt terrible – she felt like she had the biggest hole in her stomach. Everything had gone so well the last two days, but she did not see how she and Nicholas would succeed this time. As each member of her family went to their rooms to prepare for bed, Aemilia kept pacing by the windows, hoping to see the guards go home and hoping that she could still go out and meet Nicholas.

She replayed the events of the last couple of days over and over in her head. She kept telling herself that she should have brought all 10,000 denarii back to the house yesterday, but always remembered that would have been impossible.

"I'll stay up all night if I need to," she said to herself. She was determined that at some point the guards would fall asleep or give up or just assume it was too late for anyone to do anything. Then she hoped and prayed that Nicholas would still be out there, waiting on her – waiting to rescue her with the third bag of coins.

Truthfully, she doubted that the guards would leave. She doubted that she could sneak out undetected. And, she even doubted that Nicholas would be out there in the middle of the night, even if she could find a way to escape. For someone so normally even-keeled she really struggled with doubt and she felt hope slipping through her fingers. After staying at the living room window for about an hour, Aemilia sadly retreated to her bedroom.

*** *** *** *** *** *** *** *** *** *** ***

Nicholas and Rufus let about four hours pass before putting their plan into motion. They decided that they wanted to give the neighbors a chance to go to sleep and they even hoped that Adrian and his men would give up and go home. That never happened, so they finally decided it was time to act.

Nicholas left Rufus in their scouting position and walked back around the block of the neighboring houses. A minute later Rufus could barely see Nicholas come around the corner of those houses to a house five houses down from Aemilia's house. All six houses in the row were more-or-less connected, mostly sharing common walls between them. For the most part they were all the same height, though there was about a five-foot increase in height from the third house to the fourth house. The last two houses – the fifth house and Aemilia's house – were not connected, but separated by a narrow alley.

Nicholas chose the first house, Sebastian's house, as his starting point because it had an outside stairway that twisted up to the roof. He was aware that while people might be in bed and trying to fall asleep, they might not necessarily be asleep yet. So, he was going to have to be quiet as he climbed onto the roof of Sebastian's house and quiet as he walked across the roofs from house to house.

Nicholas stood at the bottom of the twisting staircase, looking at the first house with his rope, money, and coat in hand. Nicholas set the rope and money down onto the ground and gently shook out the coat. He slipped his right arm into the coat and tried to put in the other arm, but it wouldn't go in! He stumbled for a moment, and then realized that in the dark he was putting the coat on backwards.

"What a fine job I'll do tonight if I can't even put a coat on," he thought.

Getting his clothing bearings straight, Nicholas inserted his right arm into the correct arm of the coat and smoothly put the coat on. As soon as the coat hugged against his body, Nicholas was overcome with emotion. His heart was flooded with a variety of feelings. He felt the intense responsibility of rescuing the woman he loved. He felt a strange sense of transitioning from a boy to a man – like putting on the coat represented adult responsibility and the accompanying adult actions that matter in life. He also felt a strong connection to his father – he was overwhelmed by the idea that his father wore this coat day after day while working in the barn.

Perhaps more than any other emotion, however, Nicholas felt a strong sense of purpose. It was the oddest feeling. It's not like he believed his purpose in life was to slip on a costume and sneak into people's homes. It's not like he felt a sense of purpose that defines what job you choose or even a sense of purpose that defines your core values. Rather, somewhat unexplainably, Nicholas had an overwhelming feeling of purpose that was bigger than his life – a strange, larger-meaning purpose that would persist, even from generation to generation.

Regaining his thoughts after being overcome with emotion, Nicholas grabbed the money and rope and started up the stairs of the first house. It was constructed in a way such that the rooftop was the entertaining area of the house – after all, most of these houses did not have courtyards like Nicholas's old house.

As he made his way up to the roof, it appeared that no one was home in the house. He didn't see any lights on and he didn't hear any people talking or moving about. Nevertheless, Nicholas was very conscientious about the noises he made. He stepped delicately across the roof, almost not allowing himself to breathe because his breath sounded so loud to him.

This house had some chairs and plants, as well as unlit torches. The chairs and plants were arranged under a pagoda. Coming to the edge of the first house's roof, Nicholas looked at the second house, Alex's house.

"Only five more houses to go," he thought. Then he briefly panicked as the thought occurred to him that he might accidentally deliver the money to the wrong house.

Nicholas looked ahead at the second house. Its roof was only about one foot higher than the first roof that he now stood on, though there was a small wooden privacy fence between the two houses. He could see over the fence, but he would have to find something to stand on to easily make it over the fence. It didn't look strong enough to climb on and he was afraid that he would make too much noise trying to jump over the fence.

He studied the second house carefully, not able to see if there was anyone on its roof. Standing on the first house's roof, Nicholas picked up a chair and placed it beside the privacy fence. He stepped up on the chair and gently set the bag of money and rope over the fence. He realized that he didn't have anything to step down onto so he would have to leap over the fence from the chair and hopefully land as softly as possible onto the second house's roof. He held his breath and swung his right foot in front of his body as he allowed gravity to pull his body down the other side of the fence and onto the second roof. He was as quiet as a mouse, but froze in his uncomfortable landing position, listening and watching for any indication that someone might have heard him.

Confident he was undetected, Nicholas quickly, yet cautiously, walked across the roof of this second house. It didn't have any items on it – no chairs or torches or tables – and Nicholas walked quickly to the edge of the second house and looked at the third house, Nestor's house.

The third house's roof was also empty, but it provided a couple of problems.

First, there was actually a gap between the second and third houses. It was only about a foot wide, certainly nothing to worry about. However, peering down the gap did help Nicholas realize that he was pretty far off the ground.

Second, across the way he could see that the fourth house (Theodosius's house) was about five feet taller than the third house. And, as a result, there were a few windows from the fourth house that overlooked the roof of the third house. In fact, those windows were in the wall that was connected to the third house. Nicholas didn't see any lights on in the fourth house, but the windows made him nervous. He was afraid that there were people in those rooms and that they would hear or see him as he jumped from the second house to the third house.

Before proceeding, Nicholas decided that this would be a decent chance – maybe the only chance – to peek down at the guards. He took a few steps toward the front of the second house and saw Alexander sitting on the edge of the street, talking to Adrian. Nicholas couldn't understand what they were saying, but he could only imagine the lies each man was telling the other. Neither of them were honest. He had only just learned that about Alexander, but everyone knew Adrian, the slave trader, was a greedy and overall mean man.

Nicholas tried to locate as many of the guards as he could. Once he was satisfied that none of them suspected he was on the roof, he went back to his spot overlooking the gap to the third house.

With his rope in one hand and the bag of coins in the other hand, Nicholas leapt from the second house to the third house. When he landed, he slipped on some loose rocks on the otherwise bare roof and dropped his bag of coins.

Nicholas froze with fear. In his mind, the dropped back of coins landed with a loud thud and with the undeniable sound of coins clanking against each other. He knelt in silence, not leaving the position from which he regained his balance on the third roof. He listened as intently as possible, waiting to hear guards yelling that someone was on the roof or sure that he was going to see the lights go on in the windows of the fourth house – windows that were only about 20 feet from where he stood.

Not moving for what seemed like an eternity, Nicholas didn't hear anything or see anything. He slowly stood up, realizing how cramped his muscles felt from holding them in such an awkward position. He gently picked up his dropped bag of coins and started walking toward the taller fourth house. As he walked, he realized that the only way that he had to scale the height of the fourth house was by standing on one of the window ledges of that house. Each window ledge was about two feet higher than his current roof's elevation, so that would mean he would have to pull himself up another three feet to get up onto the fourth house.

Nicholas reached the chosen window and quickly recoiled in fear. There was a man and woman asleep, just inches from the window. Nicholas was thankful that his coin bag's thud didn't wake them, but he felt it was too risky to use their window as his stepping stool onto their house's roof.

Nicholas tiptoed to the other window, looked inside the best he could, and did not see anyone inside. He wrapped his rope around the same arm that was holding his coin bag and took his free hand to grab on top of the fourth roof. With a firm hold, he stepped up onto the ledge of the window, holding the rope and heavy bag with his other arm and hand. Nicholas wasn't strong enough to set the bag full of coins up on the next roof, so he starting swinging it with his arm, giving it momentum until he was able to swing it up onto the roof.

Miraculously the bag landed on the fourth roof gracefully and barely made an audible sound. He took the rope, most of which was wrapped around his arm and placed it on the roof as well. With both hands free, Nicholas grabbed the fourth roof and was about to lift himself up onto it when he felt a tug on his dirty, brownish-red coat.

At first Nicholas thought it was caught on the window and nearly had a heart attack when he saw a young boy, perhaps just three years old, standing inside the window and tugging on his coat. Nicholas let out an audible gasp when he saw the child and was amazed that the boy was not crying out in fear of the stranger standing on his window ledge. The boy tugged again on Nicholas's coat, never said a word, and gazed intently at Nicholas.

Nicholas looked deeply into the child's eyes and felt many of the same emotions that he felt with the children in the orphanage, though this boy clearly lived in a house that belonged to a family with money and opportunity. Nevertheless, Nicholas saw in the young boy's eyes innocence and wonder – pure love and a sense of helplessness. It wasn't the type of helplessness that comes from being poor or from being disadvantaged, but rather the helplessness that all humans have when they can't fend for themselves – either they are too young or too old or even too poor.

Nicholas had compassion for the boy and was overrun with warmth. He reached up into his bag, desperately feeling the need to give the boy something, even though money was probably the last thing this boy needed. Nicholas was careful not to pull out a coin of too much value, after all, he did have to deliver 5,000 denarii to Aemilia. So, he gave the boy a small coin. The child smiled back at Nicholas and pulled his partially extended body back through the window and into his house.

Nicholas was afraid that the boy might be going to get his parents, so he quickly heaved himself up onto the fourth house's roof and picked up his coins and rope. When Nicholas picked up the coin bag, he felt it catch on something. Because he was nervous from his encounter with the boy, he tugged on the bag, felt it break free from where it was caught, and lightly sprinted across the roof.

Nicholas didn't notice that the bag had torn and a small trail of coins traced his path across the fourth roof – some big coins and some small coins, some coins worth a lot of money and some coins worth just a little money.

Nicholas reached the edge of the fourth roof which was nearly indistinguishable from the fifth roof, which belonged to his mom's friend, Alexia. He barely paused to notice that he was changing houses and in a matter of seconds lightly sprinted across the fifth roof and now stood at its edge, just a few feet from Aemilia's house.

This is the part of the plan that Nicholas and Rufus spent some time discussing when they were scouting out the houses a little bit ago. Nicholas would have to get his rope, his coins, and himself across the three-foot gap between the Alexia's house and Aemilia's house. A three-foot jump isn't very far at all – it's a jump just about any of us could make whenever we were children. The part Nicholas needed help with was with the guards below. He knew he needed to jump when they weren't looking and he was depending on Rufus to distract them.

Nicholas carefully peered over the edge of the fifth house's roof and saw two guards below him, as well as the arm of one of the guards who was helping to watch the front of the house. He could also see Rufus in the distance. Even though it was dark, Nicholas's eyes had adjusted well. Rufus's eyes had adjusted too and he had been waiting, somewhat impatiently, to catch a glimpse of Nicholas on the fifth roof, beside Aemilia's house.

Rufus was relieved when he saw his friend waiting at the roof's edge and gave Nicholas a short wave. Nicholas gave Rufus a thumbs up, their predetermined sign that Nicholas used to indicate that he was ready for the distraction.

They had talked about a few different distraction ideas. One of their first ideas was that Rufus could simply walk up to the guards and ask them for directions, but they were afraid that someone might recognize him as a person who knew Nicholas. Then, they came up with the idea that Rufus could throw rocks toward the guards, distracting them in his direction. They abandoned that plan when they remembered the times that Nicholas and Rufus played catch as kids and how terrible Rufus was with his aim. One time when they were boys, Rufus and Nicholas were throwing a ball back and forth in Nicholas's father's barn. One of Rufus's throws went way to the side of Nicholas and broke a very expensive pot that Epiphanius had just purchased as a gift for Johanna. In one of Nicholas's only lies he ever told to his parents, he told them that he threw the ball and broke the pot, protecting Rufus who would have certainly received a beating from his own father. So, when Nicholas and Rufus made their distraction plan, they ruled out Rufus throwing rocks. They figured that Rufus might very well throw the rock and make it land where the guards would be looking straight at Nicholas rather than away from Nicholas.

So, they decided that their best bet was for Rufus to call out to the guards from a distance, while remaining hidden. They never quite decided what Rufus would say, just something that would distract the guards for only a moment.

With Nicholas's thumbs-up sign given, he stepped back about ten feet from the edge of the fifth house's roof, clutching the coins and rope tightly in his hands. He heard Rufus yell out, "Hey, help me! Alexander is taking my money." It made absolutely no sense, but would confuse both the guards (and even Alexander) enough to check out its source.

Rufus quickly ran away after he yelled and Nicholas set off sprinting as well. He made four quick, large steps across the fifth roof and leapt across the gap and onto Aemilia's roof. He had no idea if the guards took the bait or if they saw him jump across the gap. He planned to act quickly in case they did see him. However, he froze for a moment, listening. He could hear voices as they ran around the corner, chasing after Rufus's voice. He did not hear any guards say anything about someone being on the roof.

Cautiously confident that he had successfully made it onto Aemilia's roof undetected, Nicholas walked quietly, yet quickly, toward the front of her house where the chimney was.

With the chimney being at the front of the house and extending up past the roof, working at the chimney exposed Nicholas to the guards below. They were returning back to their posts, unable to find the source of the mysterious voice and a little embarrassed that they had all so easily given up their posts. One guard thought he saw someone on Aemilia's roof, but Nicholas's dirty coat was just dark enough and it masked the outline of his body enough that the guard quickly looked away, surmising that he was just seeing things. Besides, it made no sense to him that someone could possibly be on the roof.

Standing behind the chimney, Nicholas looked down inside it, thankful there was no fire tonight. Even though it was mostly dark, there was just enough light inside the house that he could tell the chimney provided an unobstructed path to the floor in the living room.

Nicholas set the bag of coins and rope at his feet. He took a couple of big, deep breaths, and thought it would be best to offer up a quick prayer. He pulled out his great-grandfather's necklace from under his shirt, and holding the necklace, Nicholas prayed, "Dear God, please let this work. Please save Aemilia."

He tied the rope onto the bag of coins and slowly lowered the bag down through the chimney. As the coins went lower and lower they blocked out his ability to see the floor. After about ten seconds, the bag stopped moving and the rope slacked. Nicholas wanted to be sure the bag was on the floor and not caught on something, so he lifted the bag up a foot or two and then let it fall back down to its resting place. The bag stopped again and Nicholas was confident that it made it onto the floor.

He didn't want to leave the rope as evidence, awkwardly sticking out the top of the chimney. So, he dropped the rest of the rope down through the chimney. Looking one more time, he could barely make out that the bag was on the floor of the fireplace with the rope draped around it – he had successfully delivered the coins.

Nicholas returned to the edge of Aemilia's roof. Without the weight of the coins or the rope, he decided that he could jump across the three-foot gap without running. He just barely peeked over to see where the guards were looking. One guard was already turned the other way and another one knelt down to pick up something off the ground. Nicholas took a deep breath and leapt across the gap.

Nicholas was not interested in finding out if they saw him, so he sprinted as quietly as he could across the fifth and fourth roofs that were connected as one big roof. As he ran, he thought he saw coins glimmering on the roofs under his feet and he thought that it was ironic that he was delivering such a large sum of money to Aemilia via the roofs, while there was already money sitting around on top of these houses.

Nicholas reached the edge of the fourth house, and after looking down and deciding the little boy didn't have his parents out looking for a mysterious man in a dirty coat, Nicholas grabbed ahold of the roof's ledge and let himself down onto the third roof, this time falling in between the two windows. He quickly went across that roof, jumped onto the second roof, went across it, and practically hurdled the fence that separated that roof from the first roof. Nicholas made it to the stairway, went down the stairs, and then ran out of Aemilia's neighborhood to meet Rufus near his former house.

Nicholas was overcome with pride and joy as he jogged through the neighborhood. He had actually done it! He found a way to get the money into Aemilia's house! Now Aemilia would be saved.

*** *** *** *** *** *** *** *** *** *** ***

Inside Aemilia's house everyone except Aemilia was asleep. Aemilia never tried to fall asleep and often walked into the living room to look out the front windows to see if the guards were gone. She was still determined to leave the house in what she figured would now be a vain attempt to meet Nicholas. Neither she nor anyone else in her family heard the coins or the rope drop into the fireplace.

17 – Thursday Morning, Payment 3

    Thursday morning, Nicholas woke up at dawn. He was excited and nervous to learn the result of last night's escapade. Unfortunately, Rufus had to go to work with his father. Although Rufus also woke up first thing in the morning, he couldn't go with Nicholas to Aemilia's house.
    On this morning Nicholas figured that he would hang out at last night's scouting position to watch everything go down. He sure hoped that Aemilia's family found the money. He believed that the worst-case scenario was that if they didn't find the money, then he could run in and show it to them before Alexander took Aemilia away. Of course, he knew that running in would give up his part in it and likely get all of them thrown into jail, but he decided it could at least be a last-resort option.
    He thanked Rufus's mom once more, politely refused Rufus's dad's increasingly demanding exhortation to join them at work, and began his walk across town. Soon after he left Rufus's house he caught glimpses of Diocletian's warships in the harbor. They were an impressive and imposing sight. There were about a half dozen of them and they were quite large. However, Nicholas would be just as happy when they were gone because

war ships weren't usually in town for good reasons, despite what the town crier said yesterday.

After about a half hour Nicholas arrived outside Aemilia's house. He saw a handful of guards, but Alexander and Adrian weren't there. He figured that they must have gone home overnight and left the all-night stakeout to the other men.

Nicholas spent his time waiting, watching, and nervously anticipating what the morning would bring. He so badly wanted to let Aemilia know about the money in the fireplace, but he didn't know how he could. He was eager to see Alexander's plan foiled and eager to begin moving on with his new life – a life without his parents, his house, or a job. Putting it like that sounds depressing, but Nicholas saw it as an opportunity. Besides that, he was excited about his future with Aemilia and was growing more certain that they should even marry each other.

About an hour after Nicholas arrived, Rufus showed up.

"What are you doing here, Rufus? I thought you had to work," Nicholas whispered.

"We went to the docks and there was no work to be done. Everything is closed down for the day with Diocletian's ships here."

"Sheesh. That stinks for your dad."

"Yeah, well I don't mind the day off and they are supposed to be gone tomorrow as long as the wind is right." Rufus paused for a moment, then asked, "Anything going on here?"

"Nope, just those guards who mostly have been sitting around since I got here. I haven't seen Alexander or Adrian. I figure that they went home and slept in their beds all night."

"Hmm. Leave it to Alexander to leave the nasty work of staying up all night to someone else."

Nicholas agreed and then the boys stayed quiet, waiting and watching.

*** *** *** *** *** *** *** *** *** ***

"Everyone wake up!" Faustina yelled, waking up later than she planned.

"What is it?" Diantha was the first to speak, although Aemilia was the first daughter to the living room. Aemilia hardly slept all night and was afraid to ask why her mom was yelling. She was hopeful that somehow they would have the money, but she was more afraid of learning that they didn't.

Everyone else entered the living room while Faustina began explaining. "I woke up to start a fire to heat up this chilly house. When I threw a log into the fireplace, I hit this."

Faustina stepped aside and revealed the bag of coins and rope in the fireplace.

"It's another bag of coins!" Iris exclaimed.

"Praise God!" Stephen added.

"Where did it come from?" Iris asked.

"I have no idea!" Faustina answered.

Aemilia was speechless and confused. She had brought the first two payments into her house but spent the entire night distraught because she could not go get the third payment. Tears welled up in her eyes as she saw the bag sitting in the bottom of the fireplace. Unable to even think two words in a row, she kept repeating Nicholas's name over and over in her head – in part disbelief and in part ecstasy.

Stephen went to the fireplace to inspect it and lifted up the rope that had fallen around the bag. "It looks like someone dropped the money in through the roof."

Stephen, Faustina, and Iris were smiling and laughing. Amelia was overcome with relief and began crying, leaning into her mother's shoulder.

Diantha walked over to the bag, untied its rope, picked it up and set it down on the living room floor. As Diantha carried it, Aemilia noticed that the bag had a hole in the bottom of it.

Diantha declared, "It seems a little light. I don't know if it has enough money in it."

As if on cue, Alexander and Adrian, who had both just arrived at the house, forewent the normal pleasantry of knocking and stormed into the house with a couple of guards close behind.

"All right, it's the third day. You owe me 5,000 denarii and you can't possibly have it." He looked around the room and made eye contact with Aemilia. Pointing at her, he said, "You! Come with me!"

"Just a minute!" Stephen stepped between Alexander and Aemilia. "We do have the money! It's right here."

Stephen pointed to the bag of coins on the living room floor while pushing the rope in the fireplace off to the side with his foot, hoping Alexander wouldn't see it.

"What?! Wait! How?" Alexander was speechless. "It can't be true. Where did you get that money?" Alexander grabbed the bag and opened it up.

"It can't be…" Alexander stuttered. Looking better into the bag, he said, "This doesn't look like 5,000 denarii. Adrian, count it!"

Adrian wasn't Alexander's servant and shot Alexander a dissatisfied look, and then he complied. He set the bag on a table, dumped it out, and began counting.

Outside, Nicholas and Rufus had nearly missed Alexander and Adrian walking right by their hideout. When Alexander and Adrian arrived to Aemilia's house, they saw Adrian say something to a couple of the men and then a bunch of them barge into Aemilia's house.

"What do you think is going on?" Rufus whispered to Nicholas.

"I don't have a clue. I hope everything's OK."

"Well, they haven't come back outside yet. That could be a good thing or a bad thing. Maybe we should go in."

"No, we can't risk it. We need to stay here and wait to see what happens."

Adrian finished counting the coins and proclaimed, "4,221 denarii – it's not enough!"

"Ha!" Alexander exclaimed. Looking at Stephen, he scowled, "I don't know how you got the money, but you can keep it. The girl is mine!"

Alexander marched across the room to Aemilia, where Faustina was holding tightly onto Aemilia's arm.

"Let go! She is mine. Here is the paper – it's the law!" Alexander demanded.

Alexander grabbed Faustina's hand that was ahold of Aemilia and tossed it to the side. Although he knew Alexander was acting within the law, Stephen lunged toward Alexander to stop him.

"Wait!" Diantha yelled. "We have the rest of the money! You saw it yourself yesterday – 1,500 denarii more!"

Diantha ran to the other room and produced the other bag of money.

"It's all here – count it if you like!" Diantha said as she threw the money at Alexander.

Alexander looked at the bag and then looked up at Aemilia. "I don't care about the money! I'm taking the girl!"

He grabbed Aemilia by the arm and started pulling her outside. The two guards pinned Stephen against the wall as he yelled at Alexander to stop. Iris froze in the corner. Adrian pushed Diantha out of the way and Alexander pulled Aemilia outside.

"Stop! You can't! We have the money!" Aemilia yelled, now outside and firmly in Alexander's grasp.

Seeing the commotion, Nicholas jumped up and ran toward Aemilia, with Rufus on his heels.

"Stop Alexander! You can't do this! They have the money!" Nicholas yelled.

Alexander froze and glared at Nicholas. "I knew it was you! I'll have you thrown in jail, AND Stephen and Faustina thrown in jail! Then, just because I can, I'll sell all three girls into slavery!"

"I won't let you!" Nicholas went toward Alexander, but two other guards came and held him back.

Alexander laughed. "You foolish boy. You've lost everything, including your freedom! I'll be back with the magistrate!"

Alexander laughed and turned to drag Aemilia down the street. Adrian and a guard followed him while the other guards held back Stephen and Nicholas. Rufus looked on helplessly.

Seemingly out of nowhere, a dozen Roman soldiers rode horses around the corner and down the street, followed by 20 other soldiers on foot. They were part of Diocletian's contingent in town for the day.

The most decorated soldier (the one who must have been in charge) called out, "Where is Alexander of Myra? I have been told by the magistrate that he is here."

Alexander smiled, thinking that his day had only gotten better. He thought, "Diocletian must remember my name."

"I am Alexander of Myra," Alexander said pompously, still holding tightly onto Aemilia's arm.

The soldier replied, uncurling a scroll, "Are you Alexander of Myra, the owner of the textile business who has a contract with Emperor Diocletian?"

"Yes, yes, that's me," Alexander said a little impatiently. Then turning on his charm, he smiled at the man in charge, bowed and said, "How can I be of service?"

Reading from the scroll, the soldier replied, "'By decree of Gaius Aurelius Valerius Diocletianus, emperor of the Roman Empire, I hereby charge you with cheating the emperor, overcharging and under-delivering in the substance of wool.'" Looking up from the scroll to Alexander, the soldier said, "I place you under arrest and will take you to wait for trial in Nicomedia. Your business is hereby closed." Looking at two of his soldiers, he commanded. "Take him!"

"Wait! There must be a mistake! I didn't cheat the emperor!"

"Argue your case before the judge." The soldier in command motioned again and two soldiers grabbed Alexander and tied his hands together.

"Wait! It wasn't me!" Alexander squealed in desperation. "That boy…" he tried to point to Nicholas, "he owns the business too. It was his contract. It was his fault!"

Nicholas smiled at Alexander. "Nice try Alexander. In your own words, 'You own nothing of this business. It's all mine. All mine!' Besides, I read the notice at the Court of Records – the entire thing is yours including, and I quote, 'all assets and *all debts*,'" Nicholas emphasized the last two words.

Alexander looked at Nicholas in shock, then turned to Adrian. "Adrian help me!"

Adrian looked at Alexander and then at the soldiers. "I know him, but I'm not with him." He turned back to Alexander, "Sorry, Alexander! This one is your problem."

Adrian motioned to his hired guards and they all quickly left. Adrian did not want any part of getting caught and going to jail, especially for something that wasn't even his own scheme. The soldiers turned around and took Alexander away.

Stephen, Faustina, Diantha, Iris, Aemilia, Nicholas, and Rufus all froze in place, watching the soldiers march away. "What just happened?" Iris asked.

"Oh Nick!" Aemilia ran over to Nicholas and embraced him. "I was so scared!"

"It's OK, Aemilia. It's all over."

Stephen walked over to Faustina and placed his arm around her. "Yes, praise God. It's all over. I can't believe it. It really is all over."

Nicholas, seemingly oblivious to everyone else, looked at Aemilia and said, "Aemilia, I was afraid I was going to lose you. I don't ever want to feel that way again. I know we have a lot to figure out, but I love you."

"I love you too, Nick."

Unfazed by her daughter's proclamation of love to a boy, Stephen walked over to Nicholas and asked, "Nicholas, did you have anything to do with these bags of coins?"

"Of course not," Nicholas replied. "That would be illegal." Nicholas smirked as he spoke.

"Well, perhaps the last bag belongs to you." Stephen started to go back to the house to get the last bag of coins.

"Please don't, sir. Keep it. Resurrect your pottery business. I'll be fine." Then looking at Aemilia he laughed and said, "Besides, one of your daughters might need a dowry in the near future!"

Everyone laughed. Stephen said, "Well, things might be moving a little quickly, but let's give it some time and I think this might be an idea I can support."

Stephen, Faustina, Diantha, and Iris went back into their house, crying and laughing. Rufus gave his two friends a hug and said he wanted to catch up to the soldiers and watch what they did with Alexander. Nicholas and Aemilia were alone.

"Thank you, Nick. I owe you everything."

"You owe me nothing, Aemilia. I had to do it. I wanted to do it."

"Now what, Nick? What are you going to do now?"

"For starters, I think I can get my old house back!" Nicholas laughed. "Then, I need to make another trip to the cabin to collect the rest of the money. After that, who knows? I'm thinking about becoming a priest."

"You'd make a great priest, Nick."

"Thanks, Aemilia. But, you know, I don't want to do it alone."

Then, as if he had rehearsed his father's speech over and over, Nicholas declared, "I may not be old and wise, and I may not be rich and strong. But, I want to grow old with you, learn the wisdom that comes with being loved by you, gain riches in your beauty, and build strength in your devotion and compassion. Aemilia, will you marry me?"

"Yes!" Aemilia said, tears in her eyes as she embraced Nicholas.

Then, hand in hand, they walked into Aemilia's house to celebrate with her family.

18 – The Legend Begins

There's so much more to say about Nicholas and Aemilia. For that matter, there's more to say about Rufus too. Regardless, you can bet that Nicholas and Aemilia's love continued as the happily ever after that you would expect. There were bumps along the road, but they committed to each other and loved each other until death. Nicholas did become a priest and he continued his generosity to those in need – he was even canonized as a saint many, many years later.

Before we jump to his death, however, we have a set of stories that involve Nicholas, Aemilia, Rufus, and a number of other people who you've yet to meet. Nicholas felt a strange connection to that necklace – the one his great-grandfather created. Nicholas didn't understand it yet, but that necklace had quite a meaning and Nicholas would soon begin to piece together the parts of that puzzle.

While the stories about his necklace are fantastic, they alone are not what made Nicholas into the legend that he is today. It was a legend built on his years of generosity, care, and love to those people around him. It was a legend built on his kindness to children and to beggars. It was a legend built on his kindness to people whose hope was lost and to people whose light of hope was made dim by the troubles of life.

Nicholas of Myra grew into a beloved legend between his death and the many years later when he was canonized as Saint Nicholas of Myra. It's a funny thing: the way stories become legends with a life of their own. Simple acts become great accomplishments. A nugget of truth becomes a goldmine of nearly impossible tales.

With the story of Nicholas, we have...

A generous man named Nicholas with a compassionate wife named Aemilia. A man who gave gifts to children, caring not only about their well-being but also about their happiness.

A trusted friend, Rufus, who was not quite as tall as other people, and somewhat pale – a friend who was good at making things.

A snowy retreat, separate from the world around it. A place where Nicholas could go to escape. A place where Nicholas found his resources – of faith and money and purpose.

A man wearing a brownish, red coat, dashing across the roofs.

Epiphanius and Johanna called their son Nicholas.

Both Aemilia called her husband and Rufus called his friend Nick.

Alexander jeered at him and called him the Saint of Myra.

Later in life, his parishioners called him Papa Nicholas.

The church eventually called him Saint Nicholas.

Translating the name Nicholas across languages over the centuries has evolved his name, first to Niclaus and then later to Claus.

We might actually call him Saint Claus of Myra.

But, today, many people have come to call him Santa Claus.

joedodridge.com

Did you enjoy this book? If so, then please leave a review wherever you purchased it!

BOOK REVIEWS ARE VERY IMPORTANT! – they drive the e-commerce ecosystem. Please leave an honest review.

Do you have any questions, comments, or suggestions? Contact me at
joedodridge.com/contact

Would you like free previews and updates about future books? Join my email list at
joedodridge.com/email

About the Author

My name is Joe Dodridge and I live in Fishers, Indiana. My full-time job is a high school teacher. I've taught school for 13 years and I was a pastor for 10 years. I'm married and we have two children.

I write both Christian books and travel books.

My writing "career" really started in eleventh grade when I wrote that year's first essay for English. My teacher gave me my rough draft back with over half of it crossed out and told me what I wrote was useless. I went on to get a C on that first paper and it was the beginning of a brutal boot camp experience of learning how to properly write. (split infinitive – it's OK!)

After countless papers in college and graduate school, my graduate thesis advisor was the daughter of an English professor and a journal editor. So, I went through boot camp 2.0.

In 2007, I started writing a daily devotional online. I bought a website and wrote over 150 devotionals.

Since then, I've written a lot of things that haven't made it out of my computer until July 2017 when I wrote my first book, ***A Short and Sweet Introduction to Walt Disney World Resort: 2017-2018***. That book came out of my love for Disney World, my love for travel, and my desire to finally get a book written.

Christian Books by Joe Dodridge

You Are Chased by God: a personal Bible study through the book of Jonah Understand and apply the book of Jonah to your life with this Bible study that you can use individually or in a small group.

Our Kids – Our Responsibility: weekly family Bible studies
If you're like our family, you've tried daily devotions and failed. This weekly family devotional goes more in-depth and provides an extra time just for parents.

Hold Your Breath and Jump In: a guide for the first year of college for Christians
This brief book is perfect for Christian college students to set their priorities and start college off right!

Travel Books by Joe Dodridge

A Short and Sweet Introduction to Walt Disney World Resort

400 Tips and Tricks for Walt Disney World Resort

A Look at Walt Disney World by Charts, Tables, and Graphs

A Disney World Combo Book! 3 Books in 1

A Short and Sweet Introduction to Indianapolis

A Short and Sweet Introduction to the Great American West Vacation

Manufactured by Amazon.ca
Bolton, ON